# ALL MONSTERS ARE HUMAN

An Unsettling Collection of Horror Stories

Part One of an Anthology
By Derrick Smith

# ALL MONSTERS ARE HUMAN

An Unsettling Collection of Horror Stories

Volume One

By Derrick Smith

ISBN: 979-8-9887888-6-7

Publisher:
Un-X Media
P.O. Box 1166
Independence, MO 64050

**UNXMEDIA**

**PUBLISHING**

# ACKNOWLEDGEMENTS

Beyond all else, I want to thank my family for their eternal support. My two little girls, Lily and Grace, the true meaning of my life and the only legacy of mine that will ever matter. My wife, Tara, who never says 'No, don't do that' encourages me through and through and always has my back. I would never be anywhere without you.

This project would never have come to fruition without the tireless efforts of my family. My brother, Ray, and sister, Kara, who read and reread each entry to tell me whether I was completely off-base or was on the right track. My mother, Debbie, physically printed out each and every page to check for grammar and noted when I got a little too excited and forgot a period or two. My father, Glenn, who was in the midst of purchasing a house, took the time to set aside countless hours to make sure my history was as correct as possible. My grandparents, Tom and Pauline, who had to figure out file transfers and Google Drive on the fly and worked it out with flying colors even in their golden years.

I'd be remiss if I didn't thank my close friends for making time for me starting with Iron City Paranormal, Dan and Erin, for guiding me through our incredible and sometimes unbelievable journeys to the other side. They allowed me to pursue these little ventures while inspiring me to push through long and seemingly endless hours while in between our paranormal investigations and evidence reviews, all the while tying my fictional tales of the macabre while holding true to the real-world aspects. Scott, who I'd bounce ideas off and helped inspire me and my inner darkness while sending him off on twists and turns and even questioning his own sanity at times.

All Monsters are Human

# CONTENTS

All Monsters are Human

# A NOTE TO THE READER

I've always looked toward the horror and science fiction genres as an outlet. As far back as I can remember I had a vivid imagination of dark and unspeakable terrors playing out. This would first start in my dreams as I would wake up in the middle of the night in a cold sweat. When I finally began to control them, I began to create my own narrative through my own personal movie theater, putting myself as a main character.

My mind has always been at work no matter which medium I was enjoying. I would always put my own spin or twist on a story. Eventually, during a work hiatus (I was laid off), I was finally determined to start getting my ideas on paper to share with anyone interested. After sending these quick, down and dirty writings to some friends and seeing their priceless reactions, I decided I'd venture out a little further to share them with a vaster audience.

That all culminated in this first anthology collection and realizing I wasn't alone in my crazy, dark thoughts. These tales all tie in together nicely with the title of "All Monsters Are Human." This originally hit home with me during the inaugural season of American Horror Story and led into many other aspects of life.

I believe these stories convey that deep seeded mentality for me as a person, and I hope that resonates throughout. Each story has a small part of me, my personality, or something I can relate to in some fashion. For every tale, there is a portion of my own fears portrayed onto the main character or at least a semblance of their life. I've been able to take a learning experience from some aspect of my life, as horrifying as that may sound, and turn it to some type of positive.

The overarching narrative of people being the most fearsome type of monster has certainly played some role in my own life, and I truly believe that no matter what type of monster I fall prey to, I've already faced a worse person in my past. Even though these people may not be nearly as bad or horrific as portrayed in these fictional stories, I can say without a shadow of a doubt that I know I can beat face and beat any monster that may step in my path.

Hopefully you, the reader, can take some aspect of these macabre nightmares and know that you can face anything that comes your way. You are stronger than any monster. You are stronger than any person that tries to pull you into darkness or blanket you with negativity. Your light will shine through if you let it.

Enjoy and good luck.

Derrick Smith

# DIXMONT: A DEEP, DARK HISTORY

What is now an empty field, initially planned to house a Wal-Mart, stood a magnificent but unnerving facility. Its grand, iron wrought fence surrounded the complex and the blood red brick towers rose overlooking the land around it for miles. The floor-to-ceiling picture windows allowed for generous views of the land before it became overgrown with brush. Numerous chimney stacks stretched above the roofline giving the structure an almost royal castle guise to the simple passerby. Before it was torn down, the Dixmont State Hospital (originally known as the

Department of the Insane of Pittsburgh) housed both mentally and criminally insane inmates.

When it was first opened 1862, Dixmont was of high estate, bringing in simple outcasts to society and the upper-class troubled youth. At that time, any individual was served breakfast, lunch, dinner and had coffee and pastries readily accessible at any time of day. The residents provided in-house duties such as ground maintenance, cooking responsibility, managing the coal burners, etc. Unfortunately, not even five years later the facility fell into disrepair.

The management who ran the property saw dollar signs rather than happiness and comfort for neither their populace nor the staff on hand, who was severely underpaid to say the least. The population numbers increased in this time period, specifically with the handicapped, and the staff numbers dwindled to a sole few. Needless to say, the treatment of patients was far from appropriate and acceptable, but back in that time the inhabitants were dropped off and forgotten about by society.

In 1869, less than seven years removed from it's opening and gesture to accommodate anyone in need of help and housing, Dixmont Hospital was condemned by the state after a minor upheaval by the residents resulting in the deaths of three staff members, one of whom was pregnant, and six of the residents themselves including an apparent suicide where the patient vaulted through a fourth-floor picture window.

The aftermath was brutal, and the local authorities assumed control of the patients. During this transition most of the residents were deemed mentally incapable of their own thoughts and officially handicapped. There was multiple push-backs by the inmates, whether they were confused or just disturbed, they injured two police officers and one nurse.

They liked to bite and scratch, really anything they could manage with their bare hands. Some of them were deemed insane and dangerous after these attacks; ultimately leading them to be locked in the basement.

With all of these strange occurrences, the police had no choice but to investigate during their occupation. What they discovered only lives on through local lures and folk tales. In the basement, the stench of urine and copper annihilated the investigator's senses. There were numerous electric chair type contraptions lining the walls. Instead of shocking the patients though, it appeared as though they were hooked up to a listening device of some sort and their hands would have been strapped to two metallic bars in front of them. The initial review led to a belief that anyone strapped to these machines was brainwashed with the voice recording system and a slight but steady shock running through the copper piping. The attacks were thought to be premeditated by the doctor's staff!

Once the investigation was complete and the building halfway restored to its former glory by the state, a hospital sale took place in 1873. It was to a private buyer who operated under the surname of Kirkbride. After the sale was finalized an expansion of the property occurred. The Dixmont Kirkbride building was erected to separate the inmates from the staff as a precaution and safety measure resulting in the original downfall of the estate.

Little is known about this new owner. This is mainly due to the fact that they were private sellers and, naturally, the state officials stayed far from affairs. This was intentional as they too had heard stories and refused to step foot on the property. Their representative went on record stating that they had an immediate urge to vacate the property.

No one wanted near the location. Kirkbride operated the facility under the name of Dixmont Mental Hospital and drew in crowds of nearly 400 inmates at its peak. They had no problem accepting payment from the state to hide their criminally insane and dangerous behavior. The police set up in the basement that remained intact and held the most dangerous prisoners in restrained jackets and tightly sealed rooms.

A cemetery was formally established, and a large mass was held on-site to honor all the lost souls who had perished during the last regime and a large monument was erected with all of their names and any pictures families supplied. Few family members attended, however, a large number of elected officials were in attendance, for no other reason than to show their good faith and prove that they left the hospital in good hands.

Over the next few years, the numbers of housed patients grew. More expansions took place, adding full wings on both sides of the main building, a large rotunda in the staff quarters, and a full garden in a common area complete with a pergola and hanging vines. This new management and ownership really knew how to make their population comfortable and happy.

With as much praise that this Kirkbride received, the real owner was never seen, only heard. His voice would periodically be announced over loudspeakers, ensuring that they were all in good hands and that if they needed anything to let the staff know. His office was always vacant. The lights are always off, and the door locked. Not until the facility closed down for good in 1984, with over 100 years of service by the Kirkbride family, did the public (not on record of course) find out what was truly going on beneath the surface.

All seemed well under the tutelage of the Kirkbride family. Their names were never fully revealed but according to his staff, Mr. Kirkbride was a mental disorder specialist with a focus on the brain and the nervous system while Mrs. Kirkbride was a high-powered attorney originally working in New York City. It was also well known that Mrs. Kirkbride was barren, so they adopted one child who was actually seen frolicking amongst the patients and in the wooded area on a regular basis while he was young. In due time, the young Kirkbride also disappeared right along with his parents. The head nurse speculated in her daily journal that Mr. Kirkbride wanted to pass along his life's work to someone and so he took his adopted son under his wing.

The maximum capacity for the hospital over the years was always filled as 400 occupants. The strange thing is that during those first few years in particular, the number of patients grew; and grew fast. Somehow though, that steady number of 400 occupants never wavered. The other peculiar aspect was that the dead were buried in the private cemetery, but never officially recorded in their deed book. There were never any hearses seen on-site nor were there ever any priests or church officiant spotted around the campus. Tombstones and fresh graves just seemingly appeared overnight. Before the demolition, the tombstones all read "Passed away peacefully from natural causes." I don't know about you, but those odds seem a little off that the vast array of deceased actually passed away from their natural causes.

Regardless of the strange coincidences and possible conspiracy theories attached to the asylum, the police never once stepped foot on the grounds since they gave up control upon sale. It was rumored that Mrs. Kirkbride with her well-known connections to the government and their small fortune that they had some hands in the local government pockets. But whatever the case, Dixmont remained peaceful on the surface. To the locals, the government, and staff members (who were paid much better under the Kirkbride's) that is what mattered most.

Let's fast forward to Mr. Kirkbride's passing in January of 1909. Mrs. Kirkbride refused to let him be buried on the cemetery grounds. She arranged for the doctoral board of the hospital, including the nursing corps, to escort her with her husband's body back to New York City where she planned on opening a family plot back "home" as she stated numerous times. The journey was unsuccessful as a typical Pittsburgh winter storm picked up and halted the caravan.

Mrs. Kirkbride died that same night, next to her husband. They never made it to the family plot. They were buried side by side in the Dixmont cemetery much to her disapproval.

The estate fell on the young Kirkbride's shoulders. Now, in his mid-thirties, known only as Junior Kirkbride, he made his face well known around the facility. Unlike his father before him, he wanted to be well-known and a public figure. Still, the office which was passed down to him was never used.

The inhabitant numbers slipped until they reached an all-time low for the asylum of 53 only ten years later in 1929. At this point, the patients passed away regularly but during his tenure, Junior had the deaths recorded. They varied from simple and understandable causes like infections to suicides all the way up to "surgery accidents," which seemed to be the bulk of the deaths under Junior. The families were never contacted upon deaths nor were they ever properly publicized. It was well recorded in local papers that, on multiple occasions, families came looking for their loved ones only to find out they had passed away weeks, sometimes months ago.

Once reporters and investigators started appearing, Junior began to take after his father. It didn't long for him to disappear completely, not even for his voice to be heard. In fact, Junior Kirkbride was never heard of or seen again. The head of nursing took over until her death in 1983.

In 1984, the hospital was officially condemned, and the few remaining inmates were dispersed between Mayview Hospital in Bridgeville, less than 20 miles away, and the Western Psychiatric Institute in Pittsburgh, barely 10 miles away.

The Dixmont Mental Hospital was demolished in 2006, but not before quite a few stories surfaced...


## 1992

A group of five teenagers were supposedly partying in the cemetery behind the Dixmont Mental Hospital. They had their fair share of beer and whiskey after the first win of the basketball season.

Around sunset they made their way to the abandoned hospital. They had heard stories of hauntings and paranormal activity but didn't think much of it. As they grew closer, the air drew in and seemed to smother them. Late in August should have still felt in the lower 60's that late at night. They could see their breath as they drew open the old rusty door.

The loud screech of the hinges was sure to draw some attention to them if anyone else was around. They didn't care; their voices were even louder.

As they made their way into the west wing and down the dark corridor, the smell of copper filled all of their noses. The sole girl, Jessie, within the group vomited. The four young men ran off into the darkness at that very moment.

They ran down the hallway unaware of their surroundings until they turned a corner by the original administration office converted into the lobby and froze in their tracks. A light burst on and suddenly the entire area was re-furnished. It looked brand new: bright glaze over the yellow painted walls, a red swirl on the newly marbled floor, a deep voice booming over the loudspeaker.

The boys didn't know what to do. A nurse ran by them grabbing the lead boy's arm. "Come with me, I need your help!"

All four boys, still in shock, did what she said. The nurse pushed open a blocked wall, hustled down a spiral staircase, and stood over a man in a wheelchair covered by a bloodstained cloth. The boys gathered at the base of the steps.

"Wheel him over here! Follow me! The doctor needs the specimen right away!" The nurse's voice seemed faint and echoed but not like it should have. It didn't carry like a normal voice should. It almost disappeared as her voice hit the walls. She scuttled down the hall anticipating the teens to follow her. When she noticed that they hadn't moved the nurse ran back and pushed the wheelchair herself. "Fine, I'll do it myself! The doctor will appreciate my efforts," she rambled.

The teens, still completely confused, slowly navigated down the medieval hallway using the lit torches. They finally arrived at a dimly lit room with a large operating light, which had begun to buzz and warm up, aimed at a discolored out operating table.

The nurse wheeled the clothed figure close to the table. "Here she is, doctor." She seemed almost excited, giddy even when talking to the doctor.

A deep booming voice yelled out from a dark opening in the far end of the room: "Put her on the table! We must get started immediately or we will lose all brain function!"

By this time, the boys had huddled against the back wall looking in awe as the nurse laid the figure under the cloth back and rolled it onto the table. The top portion of the cloth was cut off quickly by the nurse revealing auburn hair surrounding a shaved portion of the poor soul's head.

The saw quickly buzzed around the skull, shredding the skin and mangling the skull enough to remove it. During this entire process, the teen boys now completely sober from the shock listened to the screams echo throughout the room. Blood sprayed everywhere including their sweaty game jerseys.

A broad-shouldered man sauntered out from the darkness. A black surgical mask was draped over his face, blood stains were strewn across his apron. This surgeon held a blade to the boys. "Here!" he proclaimed, "Let me teach you!"

He held it out until one of the boys hesitantly grabbed it out of his hand. It was cold, freezing cold, burning cold. The boy tried to drop the knife but could not. The rest gathered around him.

The doctor guided his hand to the bald head. He removed the top portion of the skull revealing a bright red mucus covering. With a quick swipe of his hand the mucus was gone; in its place was the interweaving of a thick pink membrane – the brain. The boy with the knife turned away and let loose a long stream of vomit.

A deep laugh echoed throughout the room. The doctor snatched the knife out of his hand. "Here, this is how you do it!" He sunk the blade deep within the brain. The doctor dug around until he pulled out a small portion of the brain and held it up. "Who wants to hold it?"

The teens pushed backward again as the doctor stepped closer. A low moan could be heard under the cloth. All the boys could do is stare at the shuddering body.

"Should I put her out of her misery?" the nurse quietly asked from behind the surgeon.

He turned his head back to the table. "Let her be. It'll be over soon. Let me complete my operation."

The shuddering persisted as the boys stared on. Finally, as the doctor backed away, the cloth slid off the cadaver – the boys slumped in fear in the far corner.

Three of the boys are still in jail for murdering their good friend Jessie. The last boy committed suicide with a surgical knife before the police could arrive.

## 2001

With all of the rumors surrounding the large property, it was surprising that a contracting company would want to restore it to its former glory, but apparently, they had a big-time buyer from the Boston area who wanted to return to his hometown after making millions.

The plan was to incorporate a sporting area in the basement – a basketball hoop, hockey net and small pool. He was also a paintball enthusiast and wished to construct a paintball field in the courtyard area.

They broke ground in the early spring months so they could get as much completed on the outside as possible, work through summer and fall, and avoid working outside during the brutal winter months.

At first, the workers just had strange feelings. The air was best described by the foreman when interviewed for a local paper as heavy. Every construction worker on that site felt a darkness surrounding the place.

The incidents started as innocent even childish pranks at first. Buckets of tools would tip over, electrical cords would be unplugged, even cars would turn on and off randomly throughout the day. To stay relaxed and focused, the workers blamed these mysterious anomalies on a playful spirit they aptly named Junior after the Kirkbride's son. Over time, they realized how bad of an idea this had been.

As work progressed into late summer, the paranormal experiences increased and reached dangerous heights. In two different situations, overhead scaffolding collapsed. Luckily, during the first accident, the overhead workers were strapped to the rooftop. The second collapse led to a severe injury of one of the crew members, even though they claim they were tied off on the roof. The rope was in perfect condition. He was hospitalized with a broken leg and fractured arm.

A dump truck carrying gravel and stone smashed into the east wing of the hospital. This crash took out a corner of the building causing the brick which was just repaired to shatter like glass, fragments burst all around the job site. Two workers were thrown off balance, one of whom slammed through an upper picture window, fracturing three vertebrae upon his fall. Bricks don't shatter like that; they crumble or smash into small bits, but shattering is just unheard of. The driver claimed the brakes gave out and would not budge. A later inspection showed that the brakes were in perfect working order.

Once the Pittsburgh storms began in early Fall, the workers made their way inside to clear out some of the remnants and debris. The taunting of Junior continued all the while. Four of these workers ventured into the basement where the murder-suicide occurred almost ten years before. Shuffling feet and whispers echoed throughout the pitch-black halls. All that lit the workers pathway was their flashlights which bounced light beams off the dank walls causing shadows to jump and bounce about. What they found down there supported local lore from the past century.

A single dark brown leather-bound journal was set under a rusted out operating table. The workers glanced through it quickly, noting the dates that stretched back to the very opening of the asylum. The word "deceased" was found 423 times throughout the book. The crew members knew immediately that they had stumbled upon something disturbing. They made a pact right then to turn in the book to the authorities…after they each took a turn skimming through it.

The remainder of the week they passed the book around, sharing stories as they went. Before they went to turn the book in, they decided to meet up one last time and share some of the most disturbing entries. The idea was to just hang around after work – that opportunity never arrived.

A sudden collapse of the east wing roof sent two men to their deaths and crushed the other two underneath the rubble. The journal was not recovered; the stories they found were shared minimally with their friends and family, who passed it onto their friends.

Two weeks later, the owner was on his way to visit the job site when he was hit with a brutal and unpredicted ice storm. He lost control and plummeted to his death. The job site was closed the following week as his heirs refused to touch the asylum.

## 2005

This leads me to my story:

It was a brisk autumn evening. I ventured to the dilapidated, worn, blood red brick building with two of my friends; Scott and Don, and Don's then girlfriend Mindi. We were skeptics, so naturally we decided to test our luck at Dixmont.

Before Dixmont, we'd been to a handful of local haunts, passed down solely by word of mouth. Turkeyfoot public pool, Aliquippa slaughter house, the Shontz residence, and the abandoned house in Economy Borough just to name a few. Aside from just getting the goosebumps and mentally scaring ourselves, we never witnessed much at any of these supposed haunts. All of this helped lead us to being more skeptics.

I can't speak for Scott or Don, but I've always wanted to find proof of some form of life after death. It wasn't until Dixmont that I truly believed.

We pulled up, cautiously approaching the estate to avoid the security guard on duty. None of us realized how close to demolition the property truly was at this point. Don got scared early on; he stayed in the car with Mindi. Scott and I just shook our heads and headed up the steep slope to the west end of the asylum.

No more than a football field away Scott stopped dead in his tracks. He threw his arm out in front of me and glanced over to me. "You don't want to do that," he acknowledged a large hole in the ground.

My face went pale as I looked down. There were three large chunks of dynamite stuffed into this hole with wire pulled out wrapping around a nearby tree. I couldn't move. "And I was expecting ghosts," I attempted my dry sense of humor.

We continued up the hill. Scott placed his hand on the rusted metal door handle. The door was already halfway open as he yanked hard. Suddenly, multiple drops of a warm, thick substance fell on his outstretched arm. Scott jerked back.

I noticed, out of my peripheral vision, shadows jumped around behind us. I shuddered and shot the flashlight at Scott's arm. It was blood! It was all over his arm. I slowly pulled the flashlight up toward his now shaking shoulders and neck line. His collar was soaked in blood.

Scott held his hand up to his nose. "It's just a bloody nose," he somehow calmly stated.

I just shook my head. I had never seen a bloody nose produce so much blood.

He simply pinched it off and attempted the door once more. The shriek of the hinges was deafening. There was no way the security guard didn't hear us.

I was on the verge of cutting and running but Scott already jumped into the building. Naturally I wasn't going to let him run into anything on his own. After all, I wanted to see something as well.

Scott pretty much ran down the hallways, shining his flashlight in each room, he just kept moving his feet past everything. I tried to keep up. I was so confused why he was moving so fast. I'm more of an explorer. I wanted to stop in every room, try to make some kind of contact with any spirit which was willing to speak to me. Instead, we flew down halls and suddenly, when it appeared that Scott was about to run into a wall, he pushed a door open. Unlike the exterior door, this door opened swiftly and quietly. I paused, and was extremely confused how he knew where to go.

No bother, I thought, he had a better handle on this place than I ever could. Before he could enter the stairwell, I grabbed his arm tight. My head was spinning. I don't know what hit me but all of a sudden I felt dazed and nauseous all at the same time. I let out a long stream of vomit and collapsed near the wall.

Scott was gone. He must have taken off down the steps. I tried to regain my balance with a hand along the stone block wall. Pieces crumbled off as I climbed back to my feet. Again, out of the corner of my eye I spotted a dash of light down the hallway.

Thinking it was Scott, I followed it, crawling over rubble and left over asylum debris. The light flashed around violently. When I drew close enough, I realized it was definitely a flashlight, but suddenly the beam stopped on me. I held my hands up to my face, the beam's light cut through my eyes.

"You!" a deep voice echoed. "Stop right there!"

I paused, still unable to see past the direct ray of light. It grew larger as it moved closer. Finally, it died completely. I felt blind. I glanced around to try to see past the spots in my eyes.

I managed to make out a large shadow just beyond the light's location. Suddenly, a tight squeeze wrapped around my arm. The light flashed back on simultaneously. I tried to pull away but the grasp tightened.

"You're coming with me, kid!" that same voice boomed again. The security guard's badge flickered in the reflection of the thrashing flashlight.

He began to drag me behind him. I pulled as hard as I could until suddenly, I slipped; my feet flew out from under me. From my upside down view I could see the guard struggle with his flashlight as it dropped behind him. I used every ounce of strength I had to shuffle back to my feet.

I sprinted away, hurdling wheelchairs, ducking under errant pipes, curling around corners. I finally paused to catch my breath. I gained the nerve to peer around the corner that I tucked behind. Nothing. I sighed a long, drawn-out breath…until I realized how lost and alone I was at that point.

"Scott!" I yelled. There was nobody, nothing to track where he went. I spun back to the way I came. Or was it the other way? Did I get spun around? How the hell did Scott know where he was going?

The only response I heard was a muffled echo, most likely that of the security guard still searching for me. I couldn't make out exactly what he was shouting but it all stopped abruptly. Strange as it seemed, I didn't feel so alone when I could hear his inaudible shouts.

Eventually, who knows how long I'd been paralyzed there, I felt my way down the block walled hallways. My eyes slightly adjusted, just enough to make out silhouettes. I still managed to step on and trip over the random debris.

Not far along my blind journey did I spot a, what at the time looked to be as bright as the sun, but in reality was a dim, flickering light right in front of me! This was not like the last light. It was not moving. It must have been the exit! Things were starting to work out!

My walking steadied. I may have tripped or stumbled once or twice but what are a few bumps and bruises to escape a haunted asylum?! I kept moving, until I drew within a hundred yards or so.

I slowed my pace to a tip toe. I'm not sure if I wanted to remain quiet or if I was in near shock. The light in fact was produced from a flashlight. This flashlight though was on the ground, in the process of dying. Above the flashlight, slowly swaying side to side in the dense breeze was the security guard. He was maybe five feet off the ground.

The noose was strung crudely around his neck up through the open rafters above the decaying ceiling. This was no accident! But how would anyone even climb that high without access?

Blood already began to collect around his neck; the guard's eyes bulged out of their sockets, and his arms swung limp by his sides. A swab of bright red blood amassed around his belt beneath an open gap of his light blue button-down shirt.

I grabbed the flashlight and swung around, not wanting to see it stitched back up! I had no words for this mind-numbing sight. My legs grew numb; I hunched over and spewed over the dead man's shoes.

I clenched the flashlight tight and started looking for signs. It was a hospital after all, even if it was decades ago. The hall was dark, pitch black. The light beam was faint and barely cut through the heavy air. I had a tingling feeling run through my spine so I spun back around. An even darker shadow, darker than the hallway, brushed past me along the wall. It turned up in the next corridor. I was paralyzed with fear. I got my proof, I don't need anymore, and I needed out – fast.

But what if that was Scott? What if he lost his mind? I panicked but I followed the shadow. I was no longer curious; I was scared, lost, and alone. What choice did I have? I took a deep breath, swallowed hard and turned the corner.

A small boy ran past me, giggling. His laughter echoed down the hallway. I spun back as I heard more feet shuffling. I glanced up at a large window where I spotted a man in all white. It definitely wasn't Scott. Were we getting pranked? Who else was here? Was I losing my mind?

He lurched close to the window; he couldn't have been more than 6 inches away from it. He looked back over his shoulder then flew backward through the opening. He was pushed by someone…or something!

All I could do was stare at this horrific scene. I pinched my eyes closed then finally glanced back down at my trembling hands holding the flashlight, the battery was dying quickly. A dark mist grew from the floor. It manifested right in front of me. It was tall, its eyes red, and it moved toward me. I swear I could make a doctor's black face mask.

I felt a tug on my shoulder. I stepped back; no, I fell backward, through a wall? No, it was a door! I was outside!

As I lay on my back, staring up at the starry sky, I couldn't help but think: was I dreaming? Did I hit my head really hard?

The flashlight was still in my hand, the blood on it was still sticky.

"Scott!" He stood right above me. "Where'd you go?! I saw some crazy shit in there!"

His face was stone cold and pale. His eyes appeared dilated and the color in them seemed faded. He handed me a dark brown, leather-bound book. I took it but didn't even acknowledge it. I tossed it in my back pocket.

He started back toward our discovered entrance to the building. I grabbed his shoulder and tried to stop him. Again, he had that unnerving fast walk. I could do nothing but follow him. I was not going back there though. In fact, I wanted to leave…I needed to leave.

Scott stopped at the entrance to the west wing. I stood down the hillside and urged him to follow me. He reached for the door; again, his nose began to bleed. Scott slumped back and held his hand up to his nose, "Shit man, I'm bleeding! Let's go back to the car."

My jaw dropped. Was it that easy? "Well thank God you didn't want to go in again! Let's get out of here!"

Now Scott was just confused. "I have no idea what you're talking about. I just want to clean this up real quick then we can head back."

I practically ran to the car, avoiding that dynamite hole. I was out of breath by the time we got back. Don and Mindi jumped out at us trying to scare us. I didn't even react. I got in the driver's seat, started the engine, and sped out of there.

Even to this day Scott claims that we never went to that asylum. He still tells me that he regrets not stepping foot on that property.

I'll never know where he disappeared to or why. I've never even brought up the book he handed over to me. The book he passed off to me contained the details of all of the deaths and barbaric operations that occurred in that dreadful place. The book that's still stashed away in my basement to this day.

The Dixmont Mental Hospital was demolished in 2006.

# THE COLLECTOR

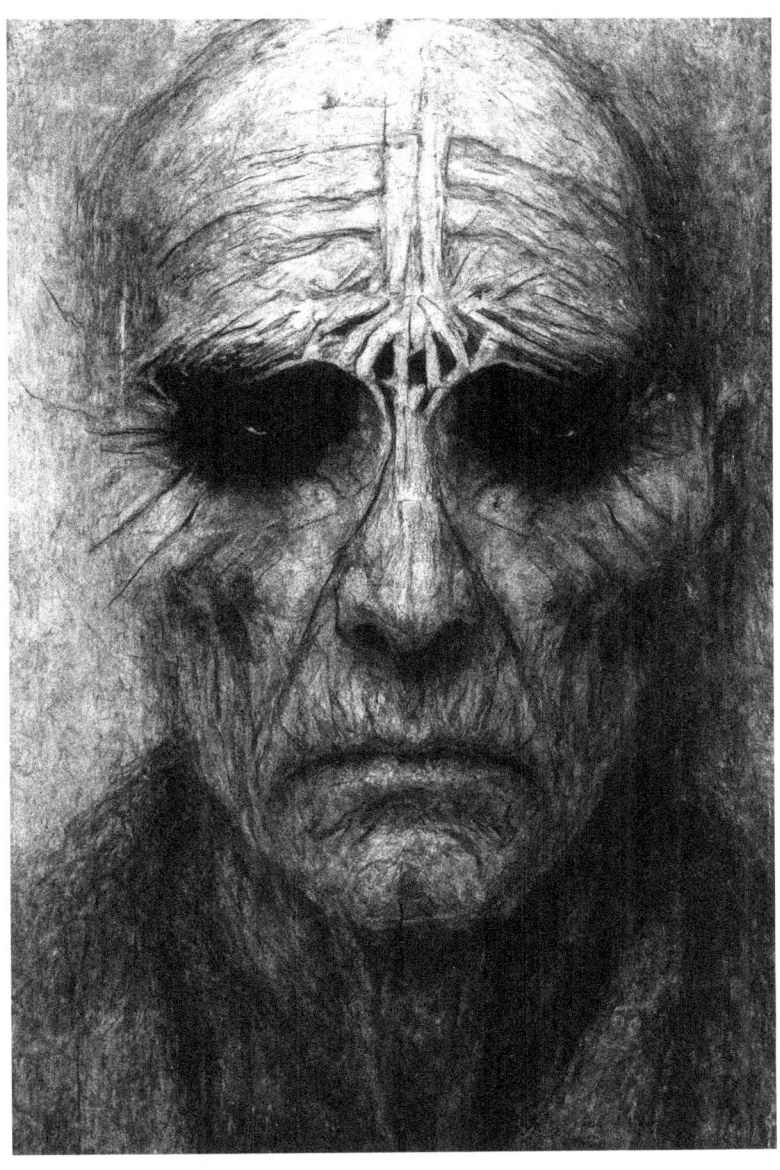

I am a collector.

My collections began with small, unimportant, irrelevant pieces. You see, I was a paranormal investigator. No, not the ones you see on TV shows. Zach Bagans is not a real investigator, he's just an actor, and not a good one might I add. I would go into properties which claimed unusual happenings would occur. Some were true, some were not, but that was the business I was drawn into. I say business loosely.

As outstanding as those cases were and how much evidence we collected, and trust me there were some doozies, I was still on much more of a skeptical level. There was no reason for this mindset, not really. I've seen a lot of unexplainable things but for some reason I just never became a true believer; at least not from these paranormal investigations.

Early on in this "career" I was given a gift of a railroad tie off of an old railway track from Martinsburg Roundhouse in West Virginia. There was nothing special about this artifact aside from its historical value. As a history buff, I thoroughly appreciated and cherished this piece of history. This was the beginning of my paranormal investigation collection.

This tradition continued on throughout years and countless investigations. Some of the more intriguing pieces of the memorabilia included things like a Ouija Board from the Archive of the Afterlife, an old book original to building from the Wexford Antiques General Store, and a bone from the Anchorage Mansion. Now, as excited as I was to receive that macabre addition to this collection, I'm unsure what or who this is from; it could be a chicken bone for all we know!

Our investigations continued but we were also constantly asked about the collection as the word made its way around the niche community. With this reputation, every location we ventured into volunteered some relic to add to the collection. My obsession began at that point to continue to add to it and even tried to push further over normal boundaries in hopes of more macabre and disturbing pieces. That was the first mistake.

## The Gun

Initially I did not pursue any relics of any nature, not even ones which fit in or were of historic value. The first time I dipped my toes into this more 'black market' collection I simply mentioned my intentions in passing to the owner of the After Hours Tattoo Shop.

After we finalized our first investigation about a month later, I received a call from this owner. He was frantic and unnerved. We seemed to uncover some deep dark secrets from the basement under his shop in relation to murders, and possibly even a serial killer from the Civil War era. He explained to me that he decided to take it upon himself to use a metal detector on the old dirt floor.

Here, he uncovered an old pistol. He wasn't entirely sure of the make or model but there was a date etched into the handle of 1864. He sent me a few pictures of it and we returned for our follow up investigation. He passed it off to me knowing of our collection during which time he did give us a warning of sorts. He explained that there was just an off-putting sensation to it and a story of a couple who were interested in getting a tattoo. They sat in the waiting area, where he temporarily displayed the weapon, only to get violently ill and were forced to leave the shop. Strangely enough, just as they exited the building their illness faded and they were completely fine. They ventured back in, after a little coercing, and as they sat back down the man got a horrible headache while the woman broke out in a strange rash right around her chest, over her heart. He wouldn't have really thought much more of this except this happened three more times.

Aside from the unnerving circumstances there was also an unspoken disappointment in losing income and clients. Following that third occurrence, he took the gun to his apartment where he kept it locked away in his safe under his nightstand. The next day, he found his cat dead with an odd bare spot on his chest and a vague explanation from the veterinarian of sudden heart failure.

He was so distraught, more like pissed off, that he actually threw the gun in the dumpster behind the pet hospital. As he arrived back at his shop, he explained that he had his phone in his hand, ready to dial us to tell us of the strange happenings. He changed his mind as he heard a loud bang from inside the shop. His first instinct was that a light blew or someone put foil in the microwave - again. He swung the door open ready to tear into an employee (he said he hoped it was the intern so he could really lay into him) but there was no one inside.

After making a quick sweep of the store, his jaw dropped and his stomach instantly twisted. That gun was laying on the table in the waiting area. There was absolutely no explanation for this and instead of telling us of these happenings, he decided at that moment he wanted to get rid of that thing.

Even though these tales were quite unsettling and disturbing I wholeheartedly accepted this offering, naturally, against the paranormal team's wishes. I kept it safe, locking it away in the storage unit, albeit nicely displaying it at the front of the metal walled room.

I thought that was the end of this strange acquisition but less than a week later I received an email to not be concerned about a police presence at the storage unit facility. I wasn't overly worried about this until the evening news explaining that a maintenance employee had a massive heart attack and died on the spot. The reporter was standing around the yellow roped off area; it was right outside my unit!

No more than a week following this unfortunate death, there was a widespread report of a cold case describing a serial killer in northern Pittsburgh. He was said to be active during the Civil War. His modus operandi was that he would poison his victims, watching them slowly suffer, then finally shooting them in the heart as one final blow knowing that it was his choice that they died when they finally perished. This was all documented in an old journal considered an heirloom to a family residing in Mars, PA. He was never captured and disappeared into Ohio, possibly leaving a wake of destruction and death in his path.

My first thought: *Is there even the slightest chance that I now owe the gun of this newly surfaced serial killer?*

**The Hat**

Following what felt like years of no vacations and barely even leaving our home in Pittsburgh, my wife and I took a much-needed vacation. Our ideal getaway always involved a beach no matter where we decided to vacation. This adventure took us to Kingston, Jamaica and this was no ordinary vacation. We stayed at a beautiful resort including food and single day excursions. This was the vacation of a lifetime, at least at first.

After a full week of relaxing and enjoying the atmosphere, the people, the time together, we wanted one last memorable adventure before our long flight back home. We had made friends with some of the bellhops and maintenance workers on the resort (mainly by tipping them nicely) so we built our nerve up to ask them about some off the resort and unsanctioned excursions.

While we failed to exploit our friendships with some of these employees, there was one younger bartender who decided to open up and help guide us through these not so friendly streets of the otherwise gorgeous island. His name was Willie and, during our walk through the small town just north of Kingston, he was called out by his nickname of "King." As we followed this King Willie we felt like he just exuded some type of energy which demanded respect. Whether it was his demeanor or his confidence we followed him without much more of a thought to it.

After entering his rusted out old coupe, we sat in the back seat in awe of the beauty of the island. The ride lasted nearly two hours but it didn't feel like anywhere near that. The partially paved roadway decreased in quality the closer we got to our destination. The gravel roadway built up and cart ruts could be seen (and felt) until the greenery opened up on both sides of us and the road seemed to just stop. The journey culminated in a gorgeous view of the onlooking ocean in the distance barricaded by a thick pure green wooded area. Immediately in front of us there were stone slabs and columns featuring shells from the ocean just barely gripping on as an old facade. This platform and foundation was clearly aged and must have been constructed centuries before anyone would have called this home, let alone the name of Jamaica.

King Willie welcomed us to the outskirts of Galina, an area which was said to be home to the first people who inhabited the island. They were said to use an ancient form of Voodoo to help bring nourishment and wealth to the island. My wife asked if there was truly gold in the island to which he cackled and explained their version of wealth was not monetary but rather in sustenance and a long, healthy life and extended family.

He dropped an arm after helping us out of the dilapidated vehicle as if to direct us toward the concrete. As we followed his lead, we noticed a bright blue light flash across the sky. We initially feared a storm which would just ruin our final day on the island. To our pure astonishment, this light occurred again and could be traced to a group of half-dressed older men forming a circle on the rocks below us. The way they manipulated this light was astounding but more so was the way they controlled a man in the middle of the group.

The chanting increased and grew into an almost hum, dull and drilling into our heads. This sensation was nothing less than encaptivating. The man in the center of the circle was much like the other men but his head was adorned with a black top hat surrounded by a slew of feathers and small bones woven into it with a silky looking fabric. He was also very old, his skin wrinkled and nearly falling from his skeletal form. This elder also wore a necklace incorporating what looked like ears from all types of animals sewn through it.

There was no way this man could move naturally in such a way. His dance (that's as close of a description as I could make of it) was reminiscent of a young child. His uncontrolled limbs swayed in unnatural rhythm with the dull humming and increased percussion of the drums. His eyes were pale blue as if he were blind and yet he danced around a fire so close that his eyebrows were smoking from the heat and close enough to the entourage of singers that they could see the yellow tinge to his teeth and the pink pockets of his gums where teeth used to be protruding.

This man's dance continued on for nearly a half hour as we were entranced by this. Eventually, King Willie convinced us to move closer to the circle, nearly becoming part of it. During this group's finale, a sudden bolt of lightning struck the ground near the man in the top hat. This blinded us for a long moment but as we regained our composure, once more in sheer amazement, this man was transformed. He was no longer an old frail man with deteriorating leathery skin and flaccid useless limbs. This man was now a young and fruitful man of no more than thirty years old.

Following this flash of light, the humming and chanting came to an abrupt end. During this period of silence, including the unnerving silence of nature, this man locked eyes with me. They were no longer the pale color of a blind man, rather they were now a gleaming yellow almost snake-like and they pierced a hole through me. Fear set in as he approached and yet my wife just looked on in awe, in a trance perhaps.

No more than a foot from me, he stared not at me but through me. A sly grin slowly grew from ear to ear. Just like moments before, another flash of light lit the entire area. The man was gone. All that remained was his black top hat still holding bone fragments and burnt feathers. The group gestured to me to pick it up as it lay at my feet. I did so reluctantly just as my wife came back from that deep trance. She too helped convince me to pick up the hat.

Reluctantly, I picked it up just as King Willie grabbed my arm, surprising me to such an extent that I jumped up and nearly out of my own shoes. He beckoned me to follow him back to his car which I had no problem following him just to get out of that rocky area. My wife wrapped her arm around mine and gingerly placed her head on my shoulder. She was humming that odd tune so lightly that I could barely make it out.

The car ride back was a blur. It should have taken another two hours but it only felt like minutes. Maybe I nodded off? I don't remember, but regardless, I was drained both mentally and physically. We exited his car back to our complex and as we walked slowly, almost at the pace of a tipsy drunk couple, my wife couldn't help but smile and tell me how wonderful of a time she had during that unplanned excursion. That was the last I ever heard her talk about it. She claims that she doesn't remember any of our final days in Jamaica.

On the plane ride home, the hat sat on my lap but during one moment when my bladder was about to burst, I left that hat on the empty seat next to me to use the facilities. Upon my return, a young child had snagged the hat from my seat and placed it on his head. Obviously much too big for him, the hat drooped down past his nose. He let out a shriek as I approached and reached for the hat. I was going to crack some kind of terrible "dad joke" but his cry took me back. Instead of a joke, I grabbed the hat and tossed it back down on the seat as he scurried off.

My wife asked why I was so brisk with him but I had no idea what she was talking about. With wide eyes and an extremely confused look, she explained that I told the child that he was disrespectful and a little brat. I apparently then made some kind of face that scared him so much that he ran off.

As I shook this notion of amnesia off, an older woman with an intense stare approached me with her young son in tow. That boy I supposedly scared off was in tears and pale as a ghost. I was scolded so much that a flight attendant had to restrain the woman. With more confusion I was eventually told by a much calmer flight attendant that the face I made was contorted so that I looked like a completely different person. Apparently, my eyes twisted from their normal circular brown state into a curved yellow variation and that my jaw had protruded so far out that it could have touched my nose.

I remembered none of that. And I tried to force that memory out of my head where it stayed - until a doctor-visit. After we arrived home and unpacked, I immediately made a trip to my storage unit where that hat has remained safely.

About a week or so following our return to normalcy, my hair began to change. It's normal brown and thinning hair with a soft texture warped into an unusual gray and thick matted mess. I made a doctor appointment as soon as I could but by the time I got into her office, my hair had completely changed with no semblance of its former appearance.

I was told that my head came into contact with some type of substance that left a residue that acted like a poison. I was asked if I had left the country or visited any type of unusual location. Obviously, the answer was yes with the Jamaican trip but what was puzzling was that residue was not just poisonous but it was also irradiated somehow.

With no answers, the doctors convinced me that my body adjusted to it and there was nothing to worry about or be concerned with long term. As long as I was okay with a very unique hair style, that would be the worst that came of it.

As I left the office with a puzzled and just overall overwhelmed sensation I held the door for an older woman and a young boy with thick gray matted hair, the same boy who put my hat on his head on the plane. He glanced back over his shoulder as I exited and we made eye contact. His yellow, reptilian looking eyes left me with nightmares for weeks.

**The Doll's Head**

This piece is just a disturbing artifact. There's no real reason behind it other than it's a dismembered doll's head with burnt hair, a broken glass eye, and a grin so unnatural that no child would have felt comfortable or happy alone in the same room with it. To top this off, it was encased inside a fogged over cracked glass box. It's situated on four thin brass legs in the semblance of clawfoot tub feet.

This was also a special piece to me as it served as the first relic I yearned for and the first I hunted down in order to add to this growing oddity collection.

Following us being sought out by a local private residence, I began to do some research on their property only to find out…nothing. Absolutely nothing happened here in the past and to add to the nothingness, the apartment complex was built five years ago and was relatively new. There was no past, no history, nothing. Normally, with lack of a past, we'd skip over this location but there was something about this location that drew us in and compelled us to investigate these supposed phenomena.

Our first visit to this residence yielded a few odd occurrences and some paranormal experiences. During our time here, there was a strong pull from this three-room apartment. The pull seemed to emanate from a small, football-sized, thick cedar box. This box was stuffed under the owner's bed and locked up tight. She explained to us that the box was here before she even moved in and just never thought much of it. We felt that there was something either inside the box or the box itself that exuded some type of energy or force. We weren't too open and honest with the girl, even though we did have some evidence and enough to write up a report. My intense draw to that box grew to such an extent that we withheld some of our findings in order to attempt a return investigation, well more like for that box.

After a rather successful follow up investigation, we had more than enough experiences and evidence to claim that the location was indeed haunted. We attempted a minor and simple cleansing of the apartment but had unwittingly asked for the box in return. She was very reluctant but eventually did come around and agreed to give us the box (as long as it didn't have hordes of money inside).

Following about three weeks of owning the box, my draw grew so intense that I threw open the storage unit's roll up door and didn't even wait for it to come to rest before I ran inside and snagged the box. That night I busted open the padlock and pried open the rusted hinges to reveal this…this…this atrocity of a baby doll.

I began to take this doll head around to our investigations but was forced to stop because of the odd trances it would put me in right in the middle of an active location. I was told I would suddenly freeze up as if I had some type of seizure and just stare at the box. What was I staring at? I guess I'll never know. But I would begin to drool and hum and just be extremely uncomfortable to be around. Obviously, this led to some failed investigations and even more canceled investigations and events.

This doll head began my wife and my split as we started to drift apart the moment I brought that head inside the house. I would just space out and completely lose track of time. Obviously, this led to our issues and ultimate failure.

Eventually I was able to manage these urges to lose control, enough so that I took the doll head with me everywhere I went. It was like my own little companion, my sidekick, my best friend. It even began to speak to me in my mind.

**The Box**

Time continued on, these pulls continued, my collection grew. Some items seemed to have an energy about them, others seemed to have some type of supernatural abilities. I was asked why I continue to grow the collection but my response is that I don't grow it. It grows naturally and on its own, it doesn't even need me.

My obsession grew so much and my means of getting these artifacts grew violent, even malevolent. This was the point my wife truly left, timed simultaneously with my exit from our paranormal team. By exit I mean the team kicking me out. My life was in shambles but I still had my collection.

This strange artifact was gifted to me years ago while working at my second job. As I picked up my paycheck, the office attendant pulled me aside knowing full well of my work in the paranormal field. She asked if I wanted this odd item which she truly could not describe with words. She explained that after her son tragically passed away of a drug overdose that she cleaned out his room months later. She stumbled upon this odd purple wax covered box. It looked like a simple jewelry box but was completely engulfed in this sticky substance.

Unaware of its true purpose or meaning, I accepted this gift. As the box was firmly in my grasp, she continued on with her story explaining that her son apparently dabbled in the occult. To what extent she did not know but she was aware that he would hold seances and meet up with other likeminded individuals.

I never felt anything odd with this box, but I did attempt some testing with it and further research. It fell into the category of a Dybbuk Box but was extremely vague in its descriptions with the symbols. The odd symbols were wiccan for the most part but they did not make much sense or match up with any typical symbology. I utilized some of my paranormal tools like K2 meters, Rempod, and Mel Meter but these devices never activated to give me any sign of anything inside. I simply tossed it in the storage unit and there it sat - until my falling out and desperation which consumed my life at that point.

One day as I was simply sitting amongst my collection, with just a dim flashlight to light the room, I heard a light knocking. It was as if my neighbor had been pounding on the separating wall. I ventured out into the hall to notice no one was around, the motion activated lights above weren't even on. Confused but not surprised, with all the energy in that room it's possible one of these pieces wanted to grab my attention. What did surprise me was where this knocking emanated from; that old Dybbuk Box. The knocking continued but grew louder with each iteration eventually drawing me to that old sealed box.

As I stood looming over this box, I still felt nothing, not even a draw to it. I snatched it up without much more of a hesitation and the knocking ceased. I truly have no idea why my next action concurred but I shook it. There was certainly something inside it that moved around but with any cursed box similar to this there should be a crystal, something of the Earth, and some inanimate object to bind the supposed spirit inside of the box to lock it inside. I shook it once more but suddenly it felt heavy. The weight increased almost to the point of me dropping it.

I placed it on the ground gently so I didn't break the seal. The knocking picked up, but grew louder and louder and louder - until a voice in the back of my mind whispered with a hiss telling me to open it. I still was hesitant to believe and, to this day with everything I've experienced on investigations and all of my odd memorabilia, I have no idea why. So, I followed my gut instinct and reached for my keys. I drug the house key (the house I was unceremoniously kicked out of) around the outside seal of the box. Each time I knocked a little more wax off creating a pile of this purple wax next to it. Finally, with one more deep scratch, the seal was broken.

Unlike with all those YouTube videos I've watched on opening these boxes nothing happened. No strange movements, no wind, no changing atmosphere, no bright lights; nothing. Instead, I opened the box slowly revealing what looked like some type of antique puzzle box. This was no ordinary wooden puzzle box, oh no, this was finished with a slick black lacquer covered in arcane symbols which were etched in a shiny golden outline.

My fingers gingerly brushed across the surface until they started moving magnificently on their own as if I had let myself go, given full control of my mind and body to my hands. As I pressed one portion of the box up, the other down, left to right, right to left, the box now transformed into different shapes and configurations but more astonishing was a sublime yet simple melody which played from an unseen mechanism. The sound was enchanting but terrifying. I wanted to stop but I could not.

Finally, I snapped the pieces into their final spots. The music stopped but now piercing my ears, and my soul, was the tolling of a bell in the distance. My final memory was that of the flash bright of a light green light.

## Souls

I have a purpose. I have a reason for my existence. A raison d'être if you will. After meeting with *them* I got all of the answers I could have ever needed. I reached the limits of reality and explored the further regions of experience. My soul was torn apart, reassembled, I was displaced from my original self and distorted beyond any believable appearance.

But still, my collection grows. It lives, it breathes, it has its own purpose for being. I add to it to this day. Whoever *they* tell me to collect, I do so without hesitation and with pleasure.

My new collection is no ordinary relic or artifact collection, hell, it's no haunted or possessed items collection. Sure, those items are still there and hold energies in that storage unit down on Smallman Street, and occasionally they like visitors but its new purpose is to house those lost souls who are unfortunate enough (or fortunate enough, depending on your perspective) to be claimed by *them*, collect by me and allowed to have their eyes open to real pleasure and pain for all eternity.

## You

And I hope that answers all of your questions as to who I am and what I'm doing here.

I'm just here to collect. Welcome!

# LOVE DRIVES YOU MAD

The two intense lights behind us drew closer. The truck's brush bar slammed up against our bumper, a strong smash jolted us forward. I kept my foot on the gas. Neither Sarah nor I wanted anything to do with those hicks.

"I told you not to get involved with those demented freaks!" Sarah shouted in my ear.

We both jerked to the right as I turned the steering wheel left. My Jetta could speed, but this was pushing it.

"Please, babe, take a breath," I tried to calm her down. "I'll get us out –"

The truck caught up beside my jet-black car. It slammed into the side of us. The front left tire gave way as sparks burst from the wheel well. Gravity threw Sarah on top of me, making me jerk the wheel. The insane driver in the green truck forced himself onto the side of us even more. Finally, the Jetta gave way. We were hurled from our seats up into the air. My car's wheels left the dirt surface of the back road and flipped over.

"I'm sorry," I whispered as we rolled with the car. Both of us were thrown like rag dolls as I blamed myself for bringing this whole encounter on in the first place.


**- One Month Ago -**


"Alright! Unemployment!" I announced sarcastically.

"So, you're buying me dinner?" she asked playfully, chuckling.

"Last paycheck, why not?" I looked down at the menu, then over to Adam. "So, how's everything going with Katie?"

He shot me a look as Sarah nudged me from the side, "Babe," she whispered.

"It's cool," he overheard her. "Seven Springs was fun. A lot of…well a lot of fun." He grinned.

Sarah shook her head, "Wasn't that expensive? I mean unless you split it, I guess it wouldn't be too bad."

Adam laughed, glancing toward me, "You haven't told her any of those stories I told you?"

I shook my head as I looked over the menu, "Who's bright idea was it to come here?

"Mine. Why?" Adam looked confused.

"Because these are some great prices," I paused. "Oh, and no I didn't tell her that Becca is cheap and makes you pay for everything."

Sarah finally reached for her menu, "Oh Der…"

"No seriously," Adam chimed in, "she is so cheap. She doesn't pay for anything. I am forced to buy everything."

"Really?" Sarah seemed shocked. "Aren't her parents loaded?"

Adam cackled, "I think Derrick asked that question." He looked over to my shoulder, "Nice, she's here."

Sarah jumped up and crawled over my lap. She threw her arms around the petite girl that hurried over to our table at Chili's. "Katie! I haven't seen you forever!"

Katie giggled as Adam and I stood from our booth. "How are you?" I asked with a smile in my voice. Adam stood quietly beside me.

"I'm fine. Work was crazy." Katie shrugged off some of the rainwater on her shoulders.

"Here, sit," Adam beckoned. He took a step back and let her into the booth.

Her cheeks flushed a little, "Thanks."

Sarah and I sat back down, "So how's Don?" I joked.

"Oh, he still doesn't realize that we're done. I mean, I took the ring off and threw it in his face. How much more does he need?" She grabbed a menu.

"What an idiot!" Adam shouted. "I mean he cheated on you with five different girls."

"Wait, five?" She was shocked.

"Didn't we tell you that?" I asked.

Sarah smiled, "We only told her about two."

"Son of a bitch!" Adam bellowed.

"You must tell - now," Katie inched closer to Adam.

He buried his head in his hands, "Crap, I didn't want you hearing that from me."

"Too late," Sarah announced. "You got to tell her now."

I just sat back waiting for some more drama to set in.

"Ugh," Adam moaned.

"Please," Katie grabbed his arm.

He grinned, "Ok, ok. Well, there was Nicole on New Year's Eve. Um…the fat one at the party he told me about. And…"

I chimed in to help him out, "Then there was Mindi over the summer. You know his ex."

Katie slammed her hand off the table, "Wow, I need to get away from him. What a…a…"

"A dickhead?" Sarah smiled.

"Exactly," Katie chuckled. She moved even closer to Adam.

After a few minutes of awkward silence, while everyone looked over their menus, Katie spoke up. "Hey guys, I have the lane reserved for nine. That's like twenty minutes."

"You guys just want to eat at the bowling alley then?" I suggested.

Sarah and Adam just shrugged their shoulders.

"Ok then," I scooted out of the booth. "Let's just hope we don't see Don and his man-crush."

"Who's that?" Sarah followed me out of the booth.

Adam got up behind Katie, "Ed. What a joke."

"No shit," Sarah laughed. "He walks around like he's got a stick up his ass."

"They're so good at MMA fighting that they don't even have to practice. They're going pro by just watching," I couldn't help but laugh at my sarcasm. "So, meet you there?" I asked Katie.

"That's fine, anyone wants to ride with me?"

Sarah began to step forward, "Maybe Adam wants to go with you." I glanced over toward him. "My back seat is a little cramped anyway."

Sarah looked up to me, "Wait, I thought –"

"I'll tell you in the car," I whispered.

"Sure, if that's ok with you, Katie," Adam stepped forward.

She swung around toward her Jeep, "Yeah definitely."

"We'll follow you then," I grabbed Sarah's hand. "I'm not sure where this place is. Do you know?"

"No, not a clue," Sarah shook her head. "So why did you want to do that?"

I smiled, unable to hold back. "Well, Adam is my friend. And Katie is your friend."

"And?" she grabbed hold of the handle.

"Think about it. It's like a puzzle. You and I match up. Then Adam and Katie match up. We're each a piece of a four-piece puzzle."

Sarah sat down in the passenger side, and then I slammed the door closed. I glanced over to the Jeep. Adam had just released Katie's hand. "Holy shit, that was quick."

I climbed into the driver's side. "So anyway, Adam has been down on Becca. Don't ask why but he's not acting like himself anymore. I think we both know Don doesn't treat Katie right. So, I figure, if we can get them together, then they'll be happier and –"

"And we'll have much better friends." Sarah smiled wide as she finished my sentence.

We followed Katie's Jeep for about fifteen minutes, she sped like crazy. I guessed that she was showing off for Adam, who likes to speed in his own right. For the entire fifteen minutes, Sarah and I discussed how great it would be to have Adam and Katie as our "couple friends."

The bowling alley is in a secluded area, surrounded by nothing but woods and out-of-sight dirt roads. The building, however, looked brand new.

"Ready to go, babe?" I looked over toward Sarah who was yawning away. Katie's Jeep was parked next to us. Adam and Katie were already inside.

"Yeah, getting up at 7:00 has been a killer these past few months." Sarah unbuckled her seatbelt as I headed around to open her door.

"What do you think they were talking about?"

"How to kill Don?" I snickered.

"I forgot about that. She still really hasn't broken it off, has she?"

I looked down as I slammed the Jetta's door, "Neither has he."

Sarah grabbed hold of my hand. "This is going to get bad, isn't it?"

"I sure as shit hope not. Either way, I won't let anything happen to you." I slung my arm around her. "Let's just enjoy a game or two of bowling, huh?"

She gave me a warm smile, "I'll try."

We walked inside and met up with Adam and Katie in the bar area.

"I'll bet Don would kill Katie if he found out about us hanging out," Adam laughed with Katie.

"Hey guys," I pulled off my jacket. "This is in an interesting area."

"Try shitty area," Sarah too pulled off her jacket.

Katie pulled up a seat. "Yeah, but it's cheap."

"I'm in the mood for some wings, wait, wait. Did you say cheap?" he asked jokingly. "That's not something I hear often."

"Unless you're referring to your mom," I smiled and pulled up two chairs.

"Thank you," Sarah sat in one of them.

"I'll pay," Adam offered. "I know Guardian just laid you off, those assholes."

I was dumbfounded, "Oh, dude, you don't have to do that."
"Don't worry," Adam explained, "I just got back, and I have some money left over."

"You do?" Sarah questioned.

He shot her a disgusted look that told us both to shut up. I knew what he wanted to do. He wanted to pay for Katie but didn't want to seem like he was jumping in too fast. After all, he only met her about a week or so ago.

"Thanks man, I really appreciate that." I took a quick glance over his shoulder and froze. "No."

Katie and Adam both seemed confused. "What is it?" Adam asked.

"It's…it's…"

"Don," Sarah whispered.

"Shit!" Adam panicked. "What do we do? Shit!"

"Calm down man. Why don't you two take off? Sarah and I can tell him we were just leaving or something."

Adam swallowed hard, "Ok. Let's go Katie." He grabbed her hand.

Katie got low and slid out right behind Adam. *Thank you*, she mouthed.

"We should say hi then take off," I murmured to Sarah. "This is not at all how I pictured this night."

Sarah grabbed her head, "Ok, but not long, I really don't –"

"Hey Don!" he looked over after catching me in his peripheral vision. "How's it going?"

His skinny but muscular figure strolled over to us. "Do you know where Katie is? I can't get hold of her."

"No man, not a clue. Sarah and I were just heading out. I haven't heard from her," I explained without hesitation.

He paused, then looked back, "Hey Ed!"

I rolled my eyes then looked down to Sarah. I could tell she was growing anxious. Her foot was pounding off the ground and her fingers were twitching. I grasped her hand, "We'll take off in a sec."

Ed hurried over, "Hey Derrick. What's up, man?"

"Not much. What are you guys doing here?"

"Well Katie usually comes here on Friday nights with some of her friends. I thought I could find her there," Don grew angry. "Let's go Ed! I want to check her house. If she's with another guy, I'm going to kill him."

"Dude, calm down, I really don't want to die before I get to kill someone," Ed publicized.

"Well guys, I got to go. It was nice seeing you," I tried to get the hell out of there.

Sarah started to worry; she backed out toward the exit.

"If I find her with someone, you know you have to help me kick his ass!"

"Not tonight man. We both need to wake up early tomorrow."

Ed reached out with an open hand, "It was good seeing you dude."

I grabbed it, I didn't want to, but I felt like I needed to be nice to these pricks. At least until we could warn Adam and Katie. "See you guys. Good luck." We hustled out the door, practically ran to the Jeep.

"Oh crap," Sarah bellowed. "They're gone."

"I'll call them," I reached for my phone and dialed his number. No answer. "Try her."

Sarah attempted calling Katie, "No answer."

"Shit.  What do we do now?"

"Well for one, we should leave.  You know they're going to be rushing out here."

As we piled into the Jetta, my phone began to ring.  It was Adam.

"Hey man, what's up?" he asked.

"Where are you guys?" I questioned.

"Katie's going to just drop me off at my dad's," he explained but sounded a little nervous. "Why?"

"Dude, Don just said he's going to Katie's! He said he's going to kill whoever she was hanging out with. You need to get hold of her!" I could tell I sounded a little anxious.

"I'll keep trying her cell too," Sarah told me.

I started the car, "Hey, can you call –" A hand slammed up against my window, I jumped a mile. I glanced outside, *Great, Don again*, I thought. I wound down the window.

"I think you forgot something," a young man in a striped bowling uniform handed me my wallet.

"You startled me, man. But thank you very much," I tried to remain calm even though my heart was jumping through my chest.

"Not a problem. Some guy in a UFC t-shirt told me you left it behind," the kid said before turning to get back to work.

I shook my head while I calmed myself down. "Wow, I thought that was…"

Sarah's face turned pale, she was staring at the wallet in my hand. "That's not your wallet."

"What are you talking about?"

She simply pointed to the middle console. My wallet sat in the same position I originally set it.

I glared at the wallet in my hand, "Then whose…is…this…" I dropped the wallet on my lap. It flipped open to reveal a Pennsylvania license. The name at the top: Adam Parker. "Oh, God!" Somehow, Don got Adam's license and decided it appropriate to make sure I knew it.

"Can we go now?" Sarah stammered.

"Yes!" I put the pedal to the metal and shot dirt from the tires as I sped out of the unpaved parking lot. "Call Adam! We need to get hold of Katie!"

## - One Month Later -

"So, it's been what? A month now?" I reached for the bill.

Sarah glanced over to me, "Do you have the money?" she whispered. I just gave her a soft smile.

"Yeah man, that first week was crazy," Adam had to shout over the clamor inside the pizza place we decided to meet up at. "Don and Becca both were practically following us."

Katie laughed and agreed, "Don't forget to mention their friends. They're both so pathetic; I mean we're not in high school anymore. They need to grow up."

The four of us had a good laugh. "Are you guys ready to go?" I shouted. "I think so," Adam concurred.

"You want to meet over at the park?" Katie questioned, referring to the community park a few minutes away.

I glanced toward Sarah. She nodded as if to agree. "Yeah, that works. We haven't hung out too much," I declared.

We ventured out to our cars, Sarah and I in the trusty Jetta and Katie and Adam in her Jeep.

"You're going to tell me what happened that one time, right?" Sarah asked softly.

I nodded as we closed our car doors, "Of course, I just didn't know if he wanted me to say anything."

We settled in and pulled on our seatbelts. I was ready to get moving until Adam knocked on my window, "Hey man, you just want to ride together to save some gas?"

"That's cool. Hop in, dude." I grinned as I looked over to Sarah. She knew what I was thinking; *Of course, they had to come. They couldn't make this easy.*

Katie and Adam climbed in the back. "Thanks, Derrick. I figure it's close enough, there's no point in wasting gas," Katie stated.

"It's no problem. I was going to suggest that anyway."

It was more or less a quiet two-minute drive, aside from the music and the occasional Don and Ed joke. As we pulled up, a large dark green truck cut us off right outside the parking lot. I laid on the horn while the driver slammed on his brakes. He finally gave way and pulled through the parking lot.

"Wow, did he cut us off just to prove that he could?" Adam scoffed.

"Who cares? He's a jerk!" Sarah fumed. I reached over and grabbed her hand, "Yeah, he's not even worth our breath." I pulled the car into the lot, passing a sign that read 'Park Closed at Sunset.' The sky was starting to get dark as I parked the car.

"Wow," Katie sounded stunned, "There's no one here."

I looked around, "Odd, but I guess most of the kids around here have grown up. I just want to toss the football around, not play in the jungle gym." I smiled and glanced over to Sarah, who still looked uneasy after the whole truck situation. "Hey, stop worrying. Just have some fun."

"Yeah, you know what happened last time you said that."

I just nodded my head. "You want to grab the football, Adam?"

He seemed hesitant, "I think we're just going to head over to the play area."

"Oh," obviously I was somewhat stunned. "Ok, well Sarah and I will still play some catch."

He reached beneath the passenger seat, "Here you go." Adam handed me the football.

"Thanks, man," I reached for my wallet and phone. "Let's go."

We all seemed to exit the Jetta simultaneously. Sarah and I headed off to the open field while Adam and Katie headed toward the jungle gym.

"Meet back here at sunset?" Katie asked.

"Works for us," Sarah agreed. She turned toward me. "So, about that night…"

I tossed her the football, "Right, right. Well, what Adam told me is what Katie told him."

"Confusing but ok," she chuckled.

"Don ended up beating Katie to her house. She pulled in as Don pulled up her road. He stormed out of his car and acted as if he was going to hit her. I guess Ed held him back. She ended up screaming at him, telling him everything he had done wrong."

Sarah stopped me, "You mean like cheating on her?" She tossed the ball to me.

"Well, it seems as though there's more to the story, but he wouldn't tell me," I said as I threw the football back.

"Like…abuse?"

I was a little hesitant, "That's my guess, yeah."

"So…that's it?"

I couldn't help but grin, "Yeah, that's it."

Sarah looked as confused as I was at first, "So it went from him killing both of them to Don getting turned away by what? Her anger?"

"Well, I also think her mom's threat of calling the cops helped a bit."

"That makes sense I guess," Sarah scratched her head. "I just –"

She was cut off by the roar of an engine. It echoed throughout the entire park area even though there was no one around. No lights shining from any car on the road. Nothing.

"Ghost car?" Adam yelled from the jungle gym.

Sarah giggled, "You want to leave?"

An engine blared from the specter once again.

"I mean the point of this was to hang out *with* them, not on our own. Plus, I'm getting a little creeped out by that noise," Sarah faltered.

I agreed, "Hey guys! You want to head out?"

"Come on," Sarah insisted, "we can at least get the car started.

"Did they hear me?"

The engine growled from a distance.

Sarah nearly panicked, "Come on babe, please?" She already had a head start on me anyway.

"Ok, right behind you." I started up the car as Adam and Katie raced up to the door.

They pulled on the handle, "Ok, let's go!" Adam shouted.

Even before the doors closed, I accelerated out of the gravel parking lot toward the restaurant to get the Jeep. About a mile down the road, the engine roared again, this time not as loud. But now a pair of extremely bright lights flashed back at the parking lot.

"I know this thing can go faster. Push it, man, I don't want to know who that is or what they want," Adam grew a little nervous.

I pushed the gas pedal a little more, "I don't know how much faster I can go. We'll be back in a minute anyway. Relax."

Sarah reached for my hand and squeezed it tight. "We'll be fine. Right?"

"Of course, they're just trying to mess with us," I assured her, along with the rest of the car.

I turned up the radio to try to drown out the growling engine. The lights, however, drew closer. "Look," I announced, "we're here!"

"About time," Katie let out a deep sigh.

I pulled around the back of the vacant building next to the restaurant. "It's just like you to park away from the building," I snickered sarcastically. "Now, let's get out of…here…" I trailed off as we pulled up to the Jeep. We were all in awe. I stopped the car while we all exited and just stared at the obliterated vehicle.

All of the Jeep's tires were slashed. The windshield was completely smashed in while the side windows were all cracked. The rear door was entirely ripped off its hinges.

"No, no, no!" Katie screamed.

The engine roared as the lights shone intensely behind the four of us. The truck screeched to a halt, leaving skid marks behind it. The driver's door blasted open; the trucker, who donned a skull mask, pointed a sleek pistol toward Adam.

"No, please. We can –" Katie was interrupted as a loud boom sounded and blood splattered on her face and white dress.

Adam dropped to the pavement. Half of his head had been blown completely off. Katie knelt to his lifeless body surrounded by a puddle of blood. Sarah and I stood in awe as the driver jumped out of the truck and snatched up Katie at her waste. He casually tossed her in the passenger seat. "Didn't know anything about this did you? No idea where she was?" The driver pulled off the skull mask and tossed it at our feet.

"Don?" Sarah murmured.

"Holy sh –" I couldn't believe it. He used to be our friend. I knew he had anger issues, but murder?  "No."

Don dashed back to the truck as Katie tried to scamper out. He reached back and slammed her with the butt end of the gun. "Sit down!"

I ran toward Sarah and grabbed her hand. "Come on!" We jumped into the car. I started the engine.

A sledge hammer crashed into the windshield. I jumped back in my seat and I pushed the car in reverse and slammed on the gas. I spun the car around out of the parking lot as we headed down the back road to the side of the restaurant.

"Sarah, call the cops!"

She grabbed her phone, "No service!"

"Ok, ok. Let's think," I tried to remain calm. "Where can we go that –" the truck's lights flashed behind us. I pushed the pedal to the floor. The car did not speed up, or Don's truck just sped up even more.

He caught up to us, slammed into the side of us as I tried to turn off at a side road. The Jetta flipped as Sarah and I went flying into the air and tossed along with the car. "I'm sorry!"

I was able to pull myself from the car. Sarah was lying beside me unconscious. I grabbed her hand as the truck pulled up. Don climbed out of the truck, but I noticed two pairs of feet. "Katie?" I stammered.

"You had no right pulling us apart!" She reached over to him and kissed him long.

They reentered the truck as Don lit a cigarette with a match. He tossed it toward the Jetta as the last thing I felt was the burning gasoline which covered my body as I watched him pull away with his middle finger in the air.

# THE BOOK

This is my suicide note.

I need you to know that I love you and would never do anything to hurt you. Instead, this is for your protection.

They're coming for me and you too and I cannot let that happen.

For the past 15 years, I have researched, memorized, and studied this book, this damn book. It was supposed to make us rich, millionaires...hell, billionaires. It would have too. We were well on our way whether you realize it or not.

Before I confuse you too much, let me backtrack. This all started long ago before we met...

---

I was right out of college working two jobs. My day job was being stuck in an office and my evening job was a simple bartender. It was a slap in the face when I realized I was making more with my bartending tips than I was with my college degree.

Not only was the money depressing but my day job felt like it locked me into a tight office with no windows, and nowhere to go. We should not live like that. We're stuck in this endless money-making void where we become zombies of society. I did it; I just worked and worked, but my mind numbed every single day.

My luck changed one night at the bar. We were slow, so slow that even our locals didn't stop in. There was one guy in our corner booth who ordered a coffee – that's it! Who orders a coffee at a bar anyway?

A bad hurricane was blowing in and most of my coworkers were getting anxious to leave. I volunteered to stay and cover the coffee drinker and lock up. I would have just gone home to my tiny apartment and listened to the storm and contemplated my life anyway; why not make a few bucks doing the same thing?

The night drew on and on and the coffee man had his head buried in a book. I tried to make some small talk with him but he was just too distracted by this oh-so-interesting book. I did get a little curious but instead of getting involved, I just sat back and watched the Bucco's' game. Luckily, they were away so there was no rain out.

When I was ready to announce the last call and lock up, I received the strangest phone call. A muffled voice, almost like the voice had a hand covering his mouth.

"Is he there?" is all the voice asked.

My natural reply was to question but instead, I asked sarcastically, "You mean the coffee guy?"

It felt like a minute or so of silence with a woman sobbing in the background. I grew concerned. I was tempted to hang up but I was too intrigued. I couldn't put down the receiver.

"Do you think this is a joke?" the voice again questioned. "Do not let him leave." Then the phone went into its stagnant buzz as the voice hung up.

I still had no idea what to make of this, but the voice was stern and convincing, and I'll admit I was taken aback. I did not want to cross whoever was on the other end of that random phone call. I did what I was asked, with no questions.

I tried to act natural. I approached the coffee man and took a seat on the opposite side of the booth. That's when I first saw it. That book. It drew me in. I'll never know why. It was a grungy brown-gray color. The cover was definitely old leather, worn at the corners. It had an old natural binding that began to tear on each end. There was one word on each side. The front cover was stamped "money" in all script lowercase lettering. The back cover was labeled in a nice cursive, almost calligraphic font and all uppercase "LIFE."

The coffee man finally looked up from the book. He laid the book down and my eyes followed it. I slowly raised my gaze. His face was worn. He couldn't have been older than 30 from his build but his face showed 70's or 80's. His skin seemed to be falling right off the bone and the bags under his eyes were so heavy they reminded me of a baseball or football player's eye black. The coffee man just stared. He finally dropped his head as a tear trickled down his cheek.

"That was them, wasn't it?" his voice raspy and his thick Pittsburghese revealed itself. To the ear, it sounded more like: "At was 'em wa'nt et?"

My eyes grew wide and my flesh crawled. I didn't speak, not a word. I just nodded. Who was "them"? More importantly, how did he know? My eyes immediately shot back to the book.

"I'll stay here. They'll take me," the coffee man said almost peacefully as if he accepted this fate in a matter of seconds. "But this book," he laid his hand over the aged book as if it were sacred; "they cannot take it."

I was drawn in right then and there. I felt like in an instant my life had meaning. Protect the book. Do not let "them" take it.

The coffee man closed it and slid it toward me. Pages were hanging out of the ends. Notes; as many note pages as there were manuscript pages. He could have made another book completely. "Do not read this." His warning was stern, and his stare locked into mine. He was going to die, and he knew it. "Burn it. Shred it. Get rid of it."

I tried to grab the book as my interest peaked. His hand, which still grasped the book, would not budge. His physical strength did not match his decrepit and worn face. I pulled again and he finally released. I almost fell back, but I caught myself with my free hand, the other clutching the book for dear life.

Before I had a chance to ask about his warning the entry bell rang as four men walked in, all covered with black trench coats and 19th century bowler hats.

The rain blew in behind them through the door. Without a word, they brushed past me not noticing my existence. I slid the book behind my back as I used the coffee man to my benefit. I stepped back through the open door fighting the rain. I spun around nearly running into a rusted-out green caravan with old wooden panels. The windows were tinted, but I heard muffled screams as the van began to shake. I sprinted to the nearest alley as I did not want to be around when those shadow men came back. My curiosity made me stop, however, as I peered my head out of the alley ever so much.

Two of the shadow men crashed through the bar door and slammed open the van doors. The crying and screaming echoed out of the van down the street. A body, seemingly a woman, flew out of the van. Her long black hair wrapped around her head as she thrashed back and forth on the concrete sidewalk. The shadow men grabbed her and threw her back into the van as if she was weightless.

The remaining two shadow men carried the battered and beaten coffee man out of the bar and tossed his lifeless body into the van. The woman's gag was let loose and the only thing I could actually make out was her screaming "Please let my son go!" before the shadow men smashed the van doors closed.

Screeching tires echoed through the street and their headlights glanced down the alley where I took shelter, obviously not from the rain as I was drenched from head to toe. But the book was safely hidden under my heavy apron.

I managed to make my way back to the bar, slowly. All the while I kept a diligent eye over my shoulder to ensure my solitude.

They never came back.

I locked up the bar but left my keys and apron never to return.

The next day, I called my day job. My 40-hour-a-week-for-minimum-pay job. Simply put, I told my boss that I quit.

That's when my life began, but also when my life began to end.

---

Looking back on it, I wasted so much time. Time I could have spent with you and our children. Time I could have spent with my parents, and my friends. Time where I could have been happy. Instead, I was obsessed. I was obsessed with answers, obsessed with money, obsessed with LIFE.

I studied that book for countless hours. It taught me so much; it gave me a fortune and a future. It gave me a life and a purpose. For 15 years I dedicated myself to this cause but where did it get me? To the end.

From the first day that I had that book, I dove head first into its mysteries. The notes that the coffee man took I easily quadrupled. I owned my own business, I held (still hold) millions in stocks, owned high-end cars, owned a dozen properties, and made so many contacts along the way. But it still has me sitting in this truck only a mile down the road from our house, our home.

I'm sorry I didn't tell you everything, but I couldn't. I knew it would only hurt you. Just look at the coffee man's family. I can only imagine that the shadow men didn't just hunt him, they took his entire family.

I can't let that happen, I'm ending it before this all leads to that.

---

I opened a business only a month after I quit my futile life. It was a corner store, just normal with a few groceries, magazines, and small items - nothing special. I hired an old war veteran to run the place and a young 16-year-old high school dropout to stock shelves and act as a cashier.

Anything that I could do to solve the riddles in that damn book I would do. I'd hide in my office in the basement or in my small 10 x 10 apartment. I taught myself some of the mathematical equations and any time I ran out of paper or room in the book I would just write on a wall or a floor. I couldn't stop and break my focus.

I was making headway. Once the codes were unlocked I understood when to make deposits, and withdrawals, which banks to trust, and which stocks to buy…it was a total puzzle but I was figuring it out.

After about a year of seclusion, and my first business ownership, I sold the corner store and purchased two small convenience stores. The book explained things. Things such as the only way to make more and expand was to lose the inconveniences of small endeavors and cut ties with the past.

That wasn't the last time I'd throw away old businesses and employees, however, I couldn't just let those two employees walk away. I did still have a conscience (at that point). So, I hired them for my next business venture. They were just happy to take the jobs (at that point) and didn't question my motives. I wasn't very personable anymore, even after those years as a bartender. That book and my research consumed me. But then you came along. That book meant less and less, and I allowed you to consume me instead.

My business plans and timing of stock purchases and sales continued to flourish, I acted like I knew what I was doing, and I felt confident, you helped that tremendously. But I still felt that I needed that damn book. It was still there in that cubby under the nightstand. It still called to me.

After we had our son, I needed the damn book again. You were enthralled with him, and rightfully so. But with that, we needed more money. I needed to support him and you. We needed a bigger house. We needed to pay for his college. That book called to me yet again.

The stocks rose and I sold and purchased more small businesses until finally I could get into the car business. Then, I broke into independent banking. All of this happened within 5 years, thanks to that book. The codes showed me the way. They told me when to buy, when to sell, when to cut losses, and when to go all in.

You were living it up with our son and your family whereas I was sneaking off in the middle of the night to study and decipher and decode. I couldn't stop. I know I never disclosed how much I made or where all the money was coming from, but I can tell you that we had enough for two lifetimes. I could have walked away easily, but I didn't. No, I couldn't. As times changed and online businesses and correspondences grew, I got my hands on some IT businesses and trades. I bought low, hired professionals, and sold high.

Oh, and before I forget, my old 16-year-old dropout and retired vet both got promoted time and time again. They became some big-time players in my enterprises – until they dug too deep and tried to break away.

One night when I was in my office with that book sprawled out on my desk, these two approached me, more like they burst into my office but I could be over-exaggerating, as you know I hate unexpected visitors.

They jumped me with questions: Where did I get my knowledge? Why did I have no training? How did I have no schooling? How could I hire and fire people with no remorse? How could I just randomly close businesses on a whim? What was I capable of?

They weren't wrong. I became more and more cold-hearted and calculated but I gave them so much. They were nobodies, nothing; they would have wound up in ditches on the side of the road. I should have cut ties with them when the book told me to.

I followed through with their fate, once more intertwining it with my own. I knew what was necessary, that book told me what needed to be done, so I just followed through. I'm not proud of it but I did it.

As the two of them crowded over me, analyzing my strategies using an old manuscript, I had to react. I gave in…or so they thought. I convinced them to come with me so that I could show and explain everything. I used my riches and power to persuade them.

We piled into my old Chevy Nova (you remember that bad boy, I know you do. We had some good times in that back seat, so don't let this tarnish those memories). We drove for what seemed like hours in silence. I pulled into the empty parking lot down at Carrie Furnace. If you remember, this was just a deserted old plant or warehouse or whatever you want to call it. It was probably around midnight and it was easy enough to dump a body in the Monongahela River.

I beckoned them to follow me. They did a little reluctantly, and about 20-25 feet behind me but followed, nonetheless. Luckily for me, without any moonlight, it was pretty easy to conceal my hunting knife. No, don't worry I never actually hunted animals, I never hid that from you. But I did put it to good use on the two of them. It's true what they say, curiosity killed the cat.

I'll spare you the details but I put them out quickly. I never thought I could do it but that book gave me confidence and helped clear my conscience.

I slit both of their throats without much of a struggle. I dumped the kid in the river and tossed that old veteran in my trunk. I drove him over the bridge into the parking lot across from Kennywood. Do you remember that old bar? Well, it was a rough bar and I used that to my advantage. His body was found the next morning in the dumpster. I'm still not 100% sure if they ever even found the kid.

Yes, I do have some remorse now, but then it was just what the book told me to do. I gave them some of the best years of their lives and if I had to take it all away from them for the sake of the book and my success, well, so be it.

That was the first time I had to commit that kind of crime. But it wasn't the last. Any time anyone got too close to my secret, to that book, I would decipher a message that would tell me to get rid of them. Every time I closed up a business and someone wanted to stick around, I had to pull the trigger. That's figurative of course, I never shot anyone. It was just too messy. I liked my hunting knife and that same spot. I think I ended up killing about 20-25 people down there. Most of the time, they didn't even see it coming.

I never actually got a liking for murder, but I knew it had to happen. I started hiring some "handymen" to do these biddings. Not because I couldn't, but rather I was afraid of losing control. I was afraid I wouldn't come home to you, to our boy. This fear really culminated after I truly did lose control. The man, I believe he was one of my cooks (I barely remember half of these employees) thought I was going to hurt his fiancé or something, so he pummeled me with a rock.

I'm sure you remember that night in the ER when I told you I fell down the stairwell and hit a few steps on the way down? Well, that was a lie.

That guy slammed the side of my head with a huge rock. I'm actually surprised he could lift it at his size. Well, I ended up seeking some vengeance here. It's the only time I took this personally, which is just another reason I started hiring these deeds out. I made the man watch his fiancé's life slip out of her as I slit her throat slowly. He cried like a little baby. I guess I don't blame him. Looking back on it, if I was forced to watch you die, I would have cried myself.

Anyway, after all this, I just couldn't take it anymore. I was done with the killing. That book knew what I was doing somehow, someway. I would hire a hitman for a few hits. After three or four murders, I would decide on an immediate action to put an end to him. I felt like I was in an endless cycle of death. I would hire another hitman to replace the last one and this rotation just continued.

Finally, I broke down. All the money and killing weren't worth it. I hid the book again. I tried to clean myself up, my business, my exploits, everything.

It didn't work. The book called to me; it urged me. I couldn't resist its temptation.

Do you remember all of those "business trips" I went on? Well, I never really went anywhere. I hid in the office's basement or up on the rooftop for days at a time. I just couldn't get enough.

Then the internet happened.

I started researching others like me. I wanted to know more. What other books like this existed? I wanted more power. I had the money but I got greedy. I wanted everything. I wanted the world.

Someone found me. I knew they traced me through my internet usage and chat rooms. All my searches caught up to me. I shouldn't have done that, but I couldn't help it.

---

The more I think about it the less I want to do this. I want to come back to you, I want to run away together; me, you, Max. We could learn to live somewhere else, together. It could be just us against the world.

But that's my problem. I don't know who in the world is coming after me. I can't allow what happened to the coffee man's family to happen to us, to you, to Max. I think it's better this way. I dug too far, dug my own grave.

All I ever wanted was a family to call my own. I couldn't ask for better. You deserve so much more. You and Max deserve to be happy, to live a good life, a safe life.

I'll be leaving you with everything I have ever made: the bank accounts, the stocks, the businesses, everything. You need to be sure to get rid of it all. Take the cash and run. Take your parents, take my parents, I don't care. I just don't want the shadow men to catch you, otherwise, this is all for nothing.

I need you to live your life to the fullest and tell Max every day that I love him. I just wish I was there more for both of you, for myself.

My first contact was an email.

At right around 3:30 AM I had an email pop up, full screen on my laptop, and just buzz endlessly. I'd never seen an email like that before and I didn't want it to wake anyone. Instead of even scanning it, I popped it open.

It was from a user simply named "WeKnow."

It was a threat. They said something along the lines of "We know where your millions have come from. We know you have been using the LIFE book for nearly 15 years. We know who you are. We know where you live. We know who sleeps next to you. We know where your son is, right now."

I slammed the laptop down and unplugged it. I was scared. Not for me, or you, or Max. I was scared for my livelihood, my secrets, my money, and my power. I don't want to sound conceited or cold-hearted but that was my first thought.

I unplugged the laptop and let it die overnight. I was awoken by another buzzing noise at right around 5:30 AM, a mere two hours later.

This time, my laptop was dead but that internal noise just kept ringing, ringing, ringing. My eyes were about to pop out of my head, and I wanted to scratch my ears right off the sides of my head. I did the only thing I could to make it stop – I opened the dead laptop.

I sunk back into bed as I saw the same email user managed to email me through a dead computer. This time, the message was much more threatening. "We know you ignored our last message. Heed this as your last warning. We will end you. We will wipe you from existence. You have no choice, concede…now."

My subconscious told me this was a dream, nothing more. But that warning…I just couldn't overlook it. I responded: "What do you want me to do?"

I tossed that book back in the safe, but it didn't last.

I conceded, I gave in; but what now? Turn me in?

There was no response for more than a week. I began to relax a little and slowly but surely got back to deciphering the codes.

The emails were done, but my next contact was the phone messages. The first was a simple message from a non-existent number. The message was the same, "We know."
I again ignored the message just like the email. At this point, I thought it was a hoax, a scam, or even a hacker. I wasn't going to fall for it.

Another week passed with no contact. Then the pictures came through.

The first picture was of me. I was in my office on the 98th floor of the Steel building downtown. There's no way anyone could have gotten that picture. Later that night, I got a picture of you, sleeping. The third picture was of Max, at school.

I couldn't go to the cops. They couldn't be allowed to dig into my business or my personal life. I was getting mad. After those emails, I was ready to back down and sell everything. But after the pictures of you and Max, let alone the picture of me with that book, I was beyond pissed. The next day I got three of my best IT gurus on that phone number. I knew that I might have to kill them after just so they wouldn't ask questions but I had no choice. None of my specialists could beat their security to trace their phone number.

The next picture I received was later that night.

Three pictures came through. Each picture showed three pairs of hands.

Then one more picture.

The three IT employees had been tied up to a chain link fence. The location actually was reminiscent of Chelsea Furnace. Their arms were pulled through the ropes. All that remained were stumps where their hands used to be. They were all still alive.

I never heard from any of them again.

Do you remember last week when you pretty much forced me to take Max to the Pittsburgh Zoo? Granted, I'm glad you did for the record (at first). But there were about 30-40 minutes where I lost Max. I thought that was the end. I thought we lost him for good. I thought the end was near for all of us.

I got a picture of him holding a gloved man's hand. He looked confused but not hurt. I tried calling the number; and I texted them multiple times. I told them I would do anything they wanted. Eventually, I got another picture of Max standing outside our car. The caption was "We can do anything we want."

I knew that was the end of this charade. I was done. I made my decision. That was the night I didn't get home until probably three or four in the morning.

Once I dropped Max back off at your parent's house, I did what the coffee man told me to do. As difficult as it was, I went back to my office, ripped all my notes out of the book, and torched it all right there in my garbage can.

Done. So, I thought.

No more than two days later, I got another picture of you. This time it was up close, right behind you at the grocery store. It was captioned, "Not enough."

I couldn't take this anymore. I was done with the games, done with the threats. I texted them back and told them, "Come get me."
So, they did.

---

I emptied out my wallet on the nightstand.

The credit cards have all been closed. The debit cards have all been consolidated into our PNC account, although I implore you to empty it into a cashier's check and move it to a separate, private, and secure account.

The stock folders are in the nightstand drawer. I did not touch them aside from changing the passwords. I have all of the necessary information there. I'd like you to transfer them to Max's name so that once he turns 18 he can control them. Just a safety thing.

I wiped and torched my laptop last night and canceled all of my email accounts. There is one left open that we share but I highly recommend you cancel that and begin your own.

The shadow men are going to try to wipe me from the history books, so I already moved all businesses in your name and created an LLC to protect you. Feel free to sell them or transfer them, whatever you like. I consolidated them all under the LLC so whatever you prefer it's under your name.

Please, please, please, get rid of everything, sell the house, and the cars, and get the hell out of town. Go live at the beach. Go to your dream place, what was it? Oak Island? Just take Max and leave. Be safe, and be happy. I love you both more than you will ever understand.

---

I was in my office when the door burst off the hinges. I had no more time than to spin and spot four men, all in dark brown trench coats and derby caps. I can't be certain if they clubbed me or stunned me or whatnot but the next thing I remembered was waking up groggy, like I was coming out of an anesthetic, in the back of some vehicle. There was a dim red light illuminating the cab and a wall full of knives, rope, baseball bats, nightsticks, and barbed wire. These guys weren't messing around.

My hands were tied and I felt every bump as my head slammed off the plastic-coated floor. I managed to inch back to the wall and sit up, trying not to get cut on any of those jagged, torturous instruments or make any noise to alert my captors.

My legs were bound, my mouth was gagged, and severe pain shot up and down my spine. I could see a small pool of dried blood where I was lying. I traced it to my side and spotted a shrewd cut up my dress shirt, still tucked into my slacks.

Another bump flung me into the air. I slammed down hard on my side. As much as I tried to hold it back, I let out a loud garbled cry of pain through the gag stuffed down my throat.

At that, the cab door smashed open, shaking the walls and vibrating those demonic tools hanging above me. A man in a dark brown trench coat and black bowler grabbed my shoulders and slammed me against the wall. I could feel the sharp instruments gouging into my back.

The dark man pulled me close. All I could manage to see were his bloodshot red eyes; the rest of his face was shielded by a black ski mask.

He had a voice altering device strapped tight under the ski mask. His voice came through muffled and deep: "Do you feel this?" He shoved his thumb into my side. I cringed, and tears rolled down my cheeks. "This is a tracking device. We will know your every move. If you do something we do not like, this fancy little tool will shock you," he tapped on my fresh wound. "And if you act against our wishes again…" he trailed off and turned back to the cab.

I pulled myself back up into a seated position. I felt around the area the dark man disturbed. There was crude stitching, something you or I could have done. But underneath it I felt a little more. I dealt with a sizzling and burning sensation, and touched what felt like a pen. It was long and thin but it pushed tightly against my wound.

A quick spark burst out of the pen and a shock ran through my body, I seized up in a plank-like position. I was hard as a rock and couldn't move for what seemed like an hour. In reality, it was a mere 30 seconds. I gasped for breath as soon as I was released from the paralysis.

The dark man laughed as he ducked back into the cab, "I wouldn't touch that if I were you."
I just glared at him. I'm not sure if I was more scared or angry that someone could so easily control me now.

"And as I was saying before you interrupted me," he removed his bowler and ski mask - the coffee man!? How?! He disappeared over 15 years ago. But he looked refreshed, young, and full of life. He was so close to death so many years ago. "We will end you," he spoke softly and gently. "But before then, we will end everything and everyone you ever loved." He slammed the door behind him, locking me in the blood-red ambiance.

---

That was only a week ago.

Since then, they closed up two of my smaller businesses. Well, I should rephrase that. They made me close up two of my smaller businesses. They also made me murder two of my top employees. I followed instructions without hesitation. The only time I disagreed, they shocked me, I seized up just like in the van. I know the next time it'll be a worse discipline – like you and Max, or my life.

Two days ago, a box showed up for me, if you recall. It was wrapped in brown paper with a string around it with "Fragile" and "Time is of the Essence" stamped on it. You delivered it to me at my office. I snatched it from you and sent you on your way. I'm sorry for that, but I thought it

76

was some sort of weapon meant to harm you. I could not (and cannot) help but do anything in my power to protect you.

I unwrapped the package, knew exactly who it was from, and fully expected it to blow up in my face.

The contents took me back. It was worse than an end – it was a new beginning. Inside folded nicely was a dark brown trench coat, a black 19th century derby hat and under that was a ski mask.

I couldn't breathe; I thought I was seizing up again. I fell back into my chair and opened my collar.

There was a simple, short and sweet note on top of it all stuck in the wrapping paper:

I had been tricked by a good friend and now no one knew where I was.
Johnny O's
3 days
Midnight
Bring new clothes

Johnny O's changed owners and names a few times in the past 15 years, but when I worked as a bartender that's exactly where I worked. These shadow men, the coffee man included, wanted this to end where it all began for me.

I couldn't do it. I couldn't just accept the end. I couldn't follow the coffee man's path. I needed to take control, like I did before when I had that book.

I need you to follow all of my instructions. I reiterate, I left them for you on the nightstand. Do not try to follow me or track me down. The shadow men already have that tracker in me and will know where I end it all.

Please, as soon as you read this, take Max and leave. Uproot and live a happy life somewhere else, anywhere. Take all the money I made for us and use it.

Run.

Leave.

Live.

I love you, forever and ever, babe.

Yours, always and forever,

Mikey

# A STEP BACKWARD

It is common knowledge that Neal Armstrong was the first man to step foot on the Moon. It would be an understatement to say that it is less common knowledge for any human to know what transpired during his, and his partner Buzz Aldrin, during their two-and-a-half-hour exploration of the lifeless satellite.

Upon practically studying Armstrong's biography (I was infatuated with space exploration), I had many questions no one could answer. He made it sound as though he and Aldrin simply jumped out of their craft, touched the Moon, and then headed home. That seems just a little odd for a supposed two-and-a-half-hour exploration if you ask me. Not to mention he did not touch on his personal life once he returned to Earth and only generically spoke of his early childhood.

Anyway, not to dwell on the details, I began asking questions; questions that no one should ask. Luckily, I *had* a friend who worked within NASA before they shut down operations. I started there; after all, he owed me a big favor.

Although hesitant, I persuaded him to help me out. During our discussion he asked me multiple times: "Are you sure you want to do this?" I don't know if it was my pride or just some naive sense of mystery but my answer never wavered. Each time I shook the question off as if it was a joke. By his expression, I should have known this was no laughing matter.

On our ride down to D.C., I endured what felt like countless hours (in reality only about an hour and a half) of awkward silences. Stupid me, I never paid attention to these little things. We entered the newly renovated training center. It was still under construction. There was also an odd heavy military presence. We entered through a small, most likely illegal, side entrance. Its industrial appearance seemed appropriate enough but the tone dampened as we ventured to the underground library. He told me only few have access to this and that it is also considered an evidence locker.

The walk down the narrow spiral stairwell and primitive stone block walls made me feel as though I was traveling through some twelfth century castle. No longer did this feel like a government controlled operational facility. I began to feel as if it was more like a medieval shelter. Maybe some sort of fallout shelter built during the Cold War? On the walls hung torches, yes torches. As I tried to keep pace, I noticed nearly rotted cell bars. This easily distracted me from the thought of torches being the only form of electricity in a government establishment. The flicker of the very dim light produced jumping shadows behind which I swear I could make out old prisoners swaying side to side in their eternal prisons.

"Why jail cells down here?" I questioned. As I expected at this point there was no response. Enemies of the State? Traitors? Your guess is as good as mine.

After a trek of nearly fifteen minutes, and silence from both my close friend and me, a bright light silhouetted the outline of a substantial oak-like door. It must have weighed twice our combined weight because the robotic arm which swung it open moaned and groaned as my friend swiped his key card over the sensor.

"Good luck and try not to be too long down here. Someone will eventually venture down," he warned with genuine fear cracking through his voice.

"You're leaving?" I asked as my heart sank.

"Yes," he croaked, "I shouldn't be here." Sweat poured from his forehead, the moisture built up around his brow as he wiped it away. "I need to leave. Please hurry."

The door would have taken my arm off if I didn't jump backward. At this point, I was in so much disbelief that I didn't even get to respond or react to the door slam. But after about a half hour of rummaging through the Stone Age library I knocked over a box on which I could barely make out the title: "The Trade of Species. July 20, 1969." Bingo! All I ever needed was the date.

I could have spent hours upon hours reading through journals, entries logs, and everything else I found tossed together in that box. I decided to get straight to the point. I grabbed an old tape reel I found stuffed at the bottom and tinkered with the old projector mounted to the thick wooden table. It was in pristine condition, again I felt like I was back in time.

Once the reel spun, my life changed. I will do the best I possibly can to explain what I witnessed:

A crude sign was held in front of the camera showing the date: 1968.

It appeared to be some sort of training base that flashed up on the screen with multiple exercises that followed.

Another sign: 1969.

Neal Armstrong acted as if he was discussing a mission or being briefed with some sort of command officer. I can only guess he was a superior wearing his medals with pride. At this point there was no sound so I cannot be sure what they spoke of.

All Monsters are Human

The next sign: July 20, 1969.

The first shot depicted Armstrong's counterpart, Buzz Aldrin, staring out at the moon after they had already landed. They just seemed to wait. His space suit was already on and ready to put to use aside from his helmet.

The camera then zoomed in to some sort of golden shimmering base plate already mounted onto the lunar surface about 100 feet from the spacecraft. All appeared calm. The camera was thrust around as a shrill blare echoed throughout the craft.

Aldrin rushed to the control panel, his hands covered his ears. He turned some knobs and clicked some dials. Suddenly a voice cracked through the radio.

"In position. Do you copy?" Then a long pause ensued with just a crackle of the radio.

Armstrong could be heard taking a deep breath behind the camera as Aldrin stared at him. Finally, Armstrong passed the camera off to Aldrin. He grabbed the microphone, clicked on a button and, "This is Neal Armstrong of Apollo 11. Please come again."

"This is President Richard M. Nixon," a voice boomed. "They are ready and in position. I repeat they are ready. Over."

Armstrong reached over into his cot and pulled out what appeared to be a photograph of his family. He stared blankly for a moment until finally kissing it and tucking it into his suit.

The President spoke through the radio just once more. "Good luck son, you are truly a hero to us all." The radio crackle died. Once again there was silence.

Aldrin placed the camera down as it fuzzed out.

As the picture focused back in, the hatch had been opened as Armstrong just touched foot on the Moon. I got goosebumps as he spoke those famous words, "This is one small step for man, one large leap for mankind…" Only it didn't end there, he was still speaking, "And our neighbors in the sky."

As Armstrong bounced out of the craft and towards that base plate, somehow it was already fastened tightly to the ground of the Moon. He grabbed the American flag. Even though he slightly struggled to place it, the flag was instantaneously sucked into the hole once he moved it directly on top.

The camera zoomed close to the flag. As it did, a large, dark blanket stretched from above the craft covering the entire area in darkness. It shook the landing craft and thrashed the camera about, producing a thick fuzz on the screen.

Aldrin apparently shut it off with a click.

An enormous gray machine covered object extended the entire projector screen as the camera turned back on. Aldrin had left the craft at this point following Armstrong, who stood motionless about 200 feet away from him. Strangely enough, Aldrin never panicked and was capable of clamping the camera still between his fingers as he documented the whole scene.

The contraption that laid in front of them clicked and beeped as lights flashed and smoke sprayed out from its underside. No more than two minutes passed before Armstrong moved closer.

Heat radiated from the machine as the heat waves construed the film in the camera. The temperature must have jumped to unexplainable levels accomplishing this in the freezing cold of space.

Aldrin focused on Armstrong's face. He stared vacantly towards Aldrin, drenched in sweat. Armstrong did not seem scared though, more like intrigued. He stepped again. As he did, his suit began to smoke. Another step. Then another. The closer he got, the more he smoked.

"Hurry!" Aldrin roared through his microphone.

It was too late. Armstrong's helmet steamed up after his face distorted and drew an apple-red complexion. He collapsed onto the surface.

The camera view dropped down toward the surface as Aldrin attempted his best Moon run. He drew closer to his partner but as he did a ringing, obviously inhuman sound burst from the machine. The camera dropped, catching Aldrin crumble to the Moon surface disoriented and confused. As it hit the ground, the camera lost focus.

As the sound subsided, the view from the Moon floor showed the machine hatch open, as large as a semi-truck, ever so silently. Although inside the opening was a single light beam, not an entire back light like you picture in most movies. It was a flashlight. Out of this gigantic machine, holding that flashlight walked a man.

His complexion was slightly darker than most humans, almost a tint of blue. His height couldn't have been more than maybe seven foot tall, even though it'd be hard to tell at that distance. And his build was somewhat bulky. Not a strong bulky, but more like pudgy, almost like he was bulging out of his skin.

After crawling toward the camera, Aldrin managed to gather his balance and ambled closer for a better look at this humanoid. Suddenly, the man with the flashlight snapped his focus toward Buzz. Aldrin froze. The bluish man immediately clicked his light off then tinkered with the remote a little more.

The remote shined a bright yellow, enough to blind the camera momentarily. When the camera focused back in on the man, his skin had begun to melt right from his bones. Showing through was a dark blue coating of muscle twisted with bone. No skin remained on its body. From the sockets its' arms were once located emerged two long, skeletal arms with piercing, sharp, elbows. The knees shot out and bent backwards in the opposite direction. Its toes grew into knives, fingers slender but strong, in a standing position the creature must have grown to nearly ten feet tall. But now, as it stood in a hunched position, it reminded me of a cheetah ready to pounce. The thing's eyes bulged from its head and slanted to the side. Its jaw dropped and ripped outward exposing at least two full rows of jagged teeth protruding from it. Two small curled horns jutted from the sides of its head.

With one swipe of its arm, the beast snatched Neal's lifeless body and began to drag him to the entrance of the machine. It glanced over its shoulder without even turning its neck as Buzz inched closer to the scene. The thing growled. What came out of its mouth sounded like some sort of high-pitched frequency which could have shaken the Moon to its core.

This noise brought upon two more similar beings, but these did not have horns like the first. They paused at the door then immediately turned to Buzz and charged.

Buzz turned back toward the ship, but in vain. He was trounced, falling forward on top of the camera, cracking the lens. He grasped it to his chest as he was mercilessly hauled into the abyss.

The camera clicked on and off as it showed the complete darkness of the hallways of the ship. All that was heard were the cries of Buzz and the growl of the great monstrosities.

It finally clicked back on. This time, the frame showed both Neal Armstrong and Buzz Aldrin strapped to two blood red metallic tables, angled straight up. Neal was apparently passed out or, if God was merciful and even still existed at this point, already dead. Both were stripped completely naked and covered in some sort of mesh netting.

Buzz squinted through his bloodied and bruised eye sockets. He looked past the camera and murmured something in a very low, unnerving tone. I couldn't completely make it out but it sounded something like, "This was supposed to be a trade, not an attack."

The foreign creatures must have understood, at least to an extent, for they responded by laughing. A blue tinted hand peered out from behind the lens and placed the camera on a nearby table and allowed it to continue to record.

The three creatures gather in frame, two beside the tables on opposite sides. The third grabbed a large device, resembling that of the top of an electric chair. It stood directly behind Buzz and placed the domed, hollow underbelly of the instrument on top of Buzz's head.

Amongst the alien chatter (clicks and buzzing noises), the brute holding the device flipped a switch in front of it. "We did," it managed to speak a deep, echoing brand of English, "One of ours for your knowledge and receptacle."

Just as it managed to force out the barely recognizable English phrase, the creature plunged a metal syringe deep into Buzz's skull, cracking and crunching its way through the bone. His eyes rolled to the back of his head revealing white emptiness as the instrument of death sucked up small particles of chunky pink residue, what I would guess to be Buzz's brain matter.

Another click sent Neal's table shooting backward, laying it down. A fourth creature shuffled in heading towards the table. This one was draped in a silver shaded cloak, knives, tubes, and syringes all stuck out of its basket it carried. Just as quickly as the machine had struck Buzz's skull, this creature propelled a small knife deep into Neal's torso followed by a clear tube.

The blue hand covered the screen. The camera was clicked off.

Jolted back to life, the camera depicted Armstrong walking on the surface of the Moon; only without a spacesuit. He walked gingerly, miss-stepping occasionally and jaunting from side to side. He made his way towards a dark Moon rock lying next to the landing craft. He pressed on its' sides and out popped a small rectangular device, resembling a mini flash drive.

"They should like this footage," Armstong announced. Armstrong fought off his own body's miscues moving to the camera, snatching it from Aldrin. He turned the camera to the craft as he filmed Aldrin mounting the steps.

Once they were securely inside and the ship was air locked, the camera was pointed out to the Moon. It spotted the flag but the ship was no longer visible out the window.

"Time to visit Earth," Aldrin proclaimed as he aimed the camera downward.

"No," Armstrong commanded off screen, "Time to go home."

The camera zoomed in through the grate under their feet. It showed a white cloth covering a blue body curled in the fetal position with a long, slender arm twitching outside of it.

"Do not fret. One should do just fine," Armstrong suggested as the camera was directed again out the window, this time it picked up Armstrong's reflection in the window. "We'll be fine and so will they," he pointed to a small crate under his cot filled with what looked like fish bags. "We will start again."

Once more, as the camera shut off, it caught his reflection in the window. This time, it picked up a slight blue tint under his eye.

The screen flashed one last time. It brought up another crude sign: "The Trade." Then it blacked out for good.

I can't exactly be sure what it feels like to be in shock, but if I was after laying witness to that, I would believe it. I couldn't move. My entire world had been shaken. Does this mean the species is starting a new colony here on Earth? Are Neal Armstrong and Buzz Aldrin still alive and…alien? I wish I could have continued my quest for answers.

As I tried the door, carrying the tape in one hand, I realized I had been locked in. At that moment, I knew I was done. I was found. There was no way to escape. I had been tricked by a good friend and now no one knows where I was.

Once the door was opened from the outside, I dropped to my knees with my hands in the air. A group of large men (were they even men?) in black helmets and riot shields burst into the room. My "I-give-up" stance didn't sway them. They smacked me with something in the head and I blacked out.

I awoke from my forced slumber in what appeared as a jail cell. I glanced outside the bars and recognized exactly where I was – the hallway on the way to the library. I tried to stick my arm out through the bars but was abruptly stunned. There was a hard surface directly in front of me. Upon further inspection I realized it was glass; most likely a two-way mirror from my experience on the opposite side.

I knew I saw people in these things using those flickering flames. Now I'm one of them. How many more are down here? Does anyone else know about this? Is it a government cover-up?

Hopefully my paper towel etched story will find its way to someone, anyone. For this is my warning to the world. We are *not* alone. There is evidence in that room. I can only pray that whoever you are that you can help. Not just help me, but all of humanity. People are not who they appear to be.

This is my warning. Heed it well.

# THE RIGHTEOUS

"Ma'am, please, you don't want to go any closer." A gruff-voiced police officer held out his arm. "It's-, well, I've never seen anything like this before." His head dropped, and his shoulders shrugged.

The woman let out a piercing shriek that echoed for what seemed like miles. She tried to push past the officer, but he pulled her back sharply enough to make her head snap back. All she could do was look on in horror as the blood leaked from the dumpster in front of her, each drop creating an endless pool of dark red ooze spreading slowly into the hospital's parking lot.

She tried again to push herself forward, into the scene. "That's my husband!" she sobbed. She saw a hand with a green ring gleaming in the sunlight. As she finally pushed past the officer, she froze in her tracks. What she saw was so horrific and grisly that bile rose up in her throat. It wasn't her husband, or not entirely. The ring encircled a finger on a hand that was just that - a hand. The rest of what lay there was unrecognizable as the man she loved.

Her hand immediately covered her rounding stomach. She looked down with tears streaming down her face. "He was going to be a father…"

-      **2 Weeks Earlier** -

There was a knock on the door.

"I'm coming, hold on," Maggie pushed herself out of the recliner and opened the screen door with a squeak. "Hi Paul," she peered out onto the porch. The summer rain beat down behind the tall man. She had always thought Paul was an exceptionally handsome man, with a chiseled jaw and

94

tousled dark hair. Despite that, Maggie had never seen him as anything more than a friendly neighbor.

He caught the door open for her when it swung off its hinges. "I told you I'd be happy to fix that for you." There was a long, quiet pause as she gazed at him, and he shrugged it off. "Anyway," he handed her a package, "I think this is yours."

She looked at it with her head cocked to one side. She reluctantly reached for it. "Thanks," Maggie said with a hint of annoyance in her voice.

"Are you okay?" Paul shifted as if he wanted to come in. "I'm sure your morning sickness isn't treating you very well in this heat."

The summer air was stifling. Of course, this was when she'd finally get pregnant. Maggie and her husband Jack had been trying for months without luck. With all of the long business trips he took, she hadn't even been able to tell him yet. He hadn't seemed to notice that she needed him now more than ever.

She slipped back behind the door, closing it abruptly in Paul's face. "You know you can't be here." Her voice turned very timid and quiet. "Anyway," Maggie noticed Paul's eyes drop to the wooden porch deck as if disappointed in himself, "I need my rest."

With a fake smile, Paul nodded, and turned to walk back, down the newly paved sidewalk and past three-story houses. As she watched through the screen her mind immediately wandered to raising a child in this ever-expanding and growing town. Most of the buildings in this neighborhood had been renovated and turned over by previous generations. She wanted to join them, to put some money into their already beautiful home but

Jack just wouldn't hear of it. No matter how persistent, or at times annoying, she was, he just wouldn't budge, claiming that this house was fine and they were increasing their value just watching the rest of the neighborhood grow.

As she slumped back in her chair, wiping away a droplet of sweat, she laid the package on the floor without much more thought.

Maggie must have dozed off, because the next thing she knew, she was startled awake by another pounding on the front door. As she huffed and struggled to get out of her chair, she shouted "What now, Paul?" She sauntered to that same open door. She squinted out through the sunlight to a dark silhouette, "Paul?"

The door burst open, fracturing the wooden frame. As she shuffled backward, she tripped over the half-built bassinet slamming, her head off of something hard and unforgiving. The last thing she remembered was that black figure, with a dark hoodie draped over their face as her world went black.

---

The flickering light wavered above her, and the smell of sulfur engulfed Maggie's senses. She slowly came to, trying to piece together what was happening to her. Footsteps thudded above her, and dust showered down all around her. As she tried to catch her breath, fear crept up inside of her for the baby inside her.

As Maggie composed herself she took note of her surroundings. Her arms were bound to a metal chair with belts, legs were tied together with a rope. The footsteps increased, pacing back and forth until she heard a door slam shut and a new pair of footsteps joining the others.

A low rumble of an argument was heard above as the footsteps then scurried toward the basement door. Suddenly, the area came into focus. Maggie peered out the small barred window. From this angle, she could see her own house! Could she actually be in…yes, she was…Paul's basement!

Now her breathing picked up and she began to panic. Why, in God's name, was she in Paul's basement!? Without any more time to comprehend this, Paul's beaten and battered body came tumbling down the stairs, landing with a loud and unsettling 'thud' at the bottom of the stairs.

"Paul!" she tried to shout, but her voice was raspy. In this same breath, Maggie coughed up a mouthful of blood. She struggled against her restraints, thrashing about, to no avail digging her straps into her wrists.

Paul inched toward her, slowly, on his forearms. He couldn't speak. One eye was inflamed, a red and white puss seeping through it. His left arm was bent behind him and his right foot was spun almost completely around at a 180-degree angle. This sight made her sick to her stomach as she vomited next to his mangled body.

The footsteps above picked up. Still, she heard two sets. 'Another body?' she thought to herself. Once more, Maggie didn't have time to collect herself or her thoughts before the footsteps again scampered toward the doorway. This time, there was no sound of an argument or any voices at all.

As the light broke through the doorway, a woman, slender in build with dirty blonde hair, slowly made her way down the creaking staircase with a vape pen hanging out of her mouth. She reached the landing, took one long puff of her water vapor, then blew it out in Paul's direction. This woman glanced back up the staircase as if awaiting her partner. As she waited, she glanced around and commented, "So this is where it all goes down, eh?" With a long pause, this woman cleared her throat and spit a wad of fluid onto the floor. She looked directly at Paul and giggled, "Sorry, Paul, but I think we should break up."

The footsteps above ended at the doorway and began to make their way down the staircase. This was the dark silhouette she noticed earlier. He reached for this woman. "So, you met Lisa." His voice sounded all too familiar.

Suddenly, he pushed back his hood as he reached the landing. He glanced back over his shoulder with a simple and very calm "Hey, honey."

"Jack?..." she trailed off, her eyes going fuzzy, her body feeling limp, as she passed out once more.

---

"So, this is how it feels, eh?" Lisa scoffed as she pushed and pulled the saw. The blood splattered across her face, dripping down to the floor. She smiled the entire time. Lisa enjoyed this.

After some more intense sawing and a combination of Lisa's laughter and Paul's shrieks of pain, a hand fell to the floor. It hit the ground with an absurd and disgusting plop, spewing blood from the now-revealed stump of flesh and bone.

"This won't hurt a little," Lisa smiled, "this will hurt a lot." She picked up the bodiless hand and slapped Paul across the face. She moved down toward his leg. Without any hesitation, she dug the rusty blade into his ankle.

While his screams pierced the night, Jack sat nearby, speaking very softly. "So…"

He trailed off as if he didn't know where to begin.

"Why are you doing this?" Maggie asked. Tears rolled down her cheeks mixing with Paul's blood on the floor. "Please!" She cried out when there was no reply from Jack.

He simply shook his head. "You two…together." The blood seemed to rush to his face. "I didn't want this. Not any of it."

She sat in utter silence. The kind of silence that you can hear. The kind that is louder than the screams of the damned. She couldn't believe this. This torture and abuse because he thought her and Paul were 'together?'

"Don't worry," Jack explained. "Paul's almost done. You'll be next."

As she contemplated this, still flabbergasted by this claim, she simply screamed at the top of her lungs, perhaps at the top of the sound barrier. No one came. This basement was soundproof, much like the rest of the neighborhood, sheltered by a stone foundation and blown insulation. "We weren't together!" She sobbed, tears and blood rolled together beneath her. "I don't understand! Why are you doing this?"

Jack slowly pushed up off his knees and oh so casually picked up a heated iron. "This…" He trailed off, steam pouring out of the iron, and pressed it against the nub which was once Paul's hand. It sizzled and hissed as Paul passed out from the immense pain. "And this…" Jack pulled back, some burnt skin still attached to the iron, and moved it toward Lisa where she just finished detaching his foot, which much like the hand, thudded to the ground with a grotesque pound. Jack pushed the iron up to the stump of his ankle forcing it to hiss once more.

She cried out, pleading, begging, near convulsing knowing that she was next.

Jack threw the iron at Maggie, clipping her shoulder and falling to the floor cutting her leg in the process. "You're a monster!" He then bent down to help Lisa to her feet, all the while flashing his badge. "You really think that I was away for work?" He took a step back. "I have been investigating these murders for months! And can you imagine my shock when I finally tracked down the man responsible for this massacre!?"

She swallowed hard. "Wait, you think that Paul did this?" Maggie gasped, still gathering herself from the immense pain. "And then you do this to him!? You're the monster, Jack!"

Lisa started to brush off the blood that stained her white shirt a dark red. "Paul has been cheating on me for months anyway. He had this coming."

"You still don't get it, do you?" Jack reached for his holster, revealing his pistol.

She looked on in disbelief. "Get what?!"

Jack and Lisa glanced at one another. "Just own up to it" Jack calmly requested.

"To what? To what?" she pleaded, tears once more stung her eyes.

Lisa punched her, hard, with a right cross. "You two have been on this killing spree for how long?!" She pulled back her again but Jack grabbed her arm. "How dare you! And in my house! In my basement!

Jack slowly bent down, enough to stare directly into her eyes. "Just admit it, I want to hear it."

Maggie's face showed pure terror mixed in with utter confusion.

If Jack didn't know any better, he would think she really had no idea he was onto her. He was so close to the truth he could smell it. Strangely enough, with the end being so near, he could physically smell a burning, yes, burning of fire and brimstone. A burning of Maggie's soul in hell for the chaos and death she caused. He didn't care, he had waited so long for this moment, and nothing else mattered. "I just don't understand why, that's what I don't understand. Tell me why!"

Maggie peered down at her feet, the blood was dripping from the mark of the iron. "I... I don't understand..."

Paul coughed, and blood spewed from his pierced lips. "It worked," he grumbled from his prone position.

Jack stepped back, and glanced first at Lisa, then toward Paul, a small sliver of fear showing in his face now.

Lisa glanced over at Jack, confused. "Wait, what?"

"Oh sweetie," Paul began, "I never cheated on you…I loved you…I adored you…" More blood seeped out, and he spat toward the pair. "And you…" he stared almost through Jack. "All the beatings, the abuse…" he coughed now, growing even weaker, "I heard about all of it, in grave detail." Paul's glare turned toward Maggie, her eyes watering, "Your wife was the perfect target."

Now Lisa fell back behind Jack. It was Jack's turn to look toward her in a perplexed state. "But all the evidence, it was both of you…together."

"Oh please, Jack" Paul scoffed with his body bokeh and bleeding. "Your wife? A murderer?" More blood spewed. He attempted a weak laugh.

Jack reached for the package laying in the corner. "Explain this." He ripped into it. "More body parts," he threw it across the floor, amputated fingers flying toward Paul. "This package was sitting next to my wife! Maggie was in the process of packaging these up to send them again!"

"No!" Maggie shouted, blood trickling down from the corner of her mouth. "Paul just brought that to me today!"

A tear broke free in Lisa's eye, "What…what…" she couldn't even finish her question, instead Lisa dropped to her knees and broke down in a full-fledged sob. "You told me they were part of it, Jack!"

"And you," Paul stared a hole through her. "I know you've been taking my money." Another long silence followed. "Did I care? Not at first."

Jack stepped forward, grabbed for his gun once more, "I have video of you two, together, plotting this twisted murder spree! How can you deny that?"

"What were we doing together?" Maggie yelled as fear and frustration warned with confusion inside her. "We talk, we vent, we bitch about our problems." After another pause, gathering herself "I don't know anything else, your case, these murders, you're insane!"

Silence ensued, no one knew where to go from there. Maggie did though, she was just biding time. Jack wasn't just imagining that smoking smell, oh no. The iron that fell to her feet was burning the rope and she had used the blood around her wrists to wiggle free. These next few moments were a blur to the entire group:

-       Maggie jumped out of the chair just as Jack had pushed back against the wall.

-       He saw her lunging and he reached toward his holster for his pistol, but she threw her body against him forcing him to drop it and it went careening across the room.

-       Lisa was still enthralled in her grief and confusion on the floor.

-       Maggie grabbed the saw at Lisa's feet and slammed the butt end into the back of her head sending her sprawling face down on the floor.

-       Jack was recovering and leaped for the gun just as she slammed the saw down into his shoulder throwing him to the floor in a puddle of blood.

She made her way back to her feet, gingerly picked up the vape pen from Lisa's pocket and took a long drag before setting back down in the metal chair to pull herself together.

---

Paul was dying. The duo never cauterized his wounds and simply burnt the dismembered extremities. In only a week, he began to see signs of infection and unknown blood loss. His face was taut and gray. He lay on his bed upstairs and quietly, almost in a whisper, asked her for a favor. "I just want vengeance…" Paul trailed off, gasping for breath.

Maggie said nothing. There was nothing left to say. Paul was vengeance. Maggie was righteous. Paul's murder spree had already become infamous, dubbed the Ohio River Killer by the media, but now they were in this mess together.

Maggie knew what needed to be done.

Lisa's body parts began appearing on street corners over a week. It began with her hand and foot; the same pair she took from Paul. Naturally, he was too weak to do the physical cutting but, out of a twisted sympathy, Maggie made sure that he was able to watch every gruesome moment. Eventually, Maggie was instructed how to amputate and ultimately removed her legs down to both knees, and Lisa's arms down to the elbows, and was even shown how to take off her ears and eyelids. Once these body parts were all severed, Paul asked to set her on the third floor, overlooking the empty streets and with a view of the hospital. As her extremities were discovered from anonymous tips, Paul's typical modus operandi, Maggie made sure she was awake to witness the entire scene. Lisa did attempt to scream and yell at the random pedestrian but every time she did, Paul would instruct Maggie to remove an additional piece of her remaining face: tongue, nose, and cheeks.

No one came looking for Lisa. She had nobody; except Paul. Now that he was about to perish, she would meet the same fate. Maggie locked Lisa, well Lisa's remaining torso, inside a small 6 x 4 steel dumpster, and rolled her right behind the hospital. The employees never seemed to pay much notice but Maggie was nice enough to face and position her to look out the hole peering at the ever-so-close emergency entrance. With no tongue, and her mouth sewn shut, Lisa was left here to pass away quietly right alongside Paul who opted to join her.

The following week Maggie made herself comfortable and prepared to tell Jack the entire story, at least as explained by Paul. Aside from this being Paul's final request, she just needed to get it off her chest to someone, anyone, and hell Jack was here and now that he was beginning to lose himself little by little so he could be her someone.

She set him up in that same metal chair and prepared him with some Tylenol and antibiotics. He would have no choice but to listen and watch and naturally not run off.

_____

It all started about a year ago. Jack began to take cases that stretched him out of state but that was okay, she needed her alone time. All the while, she befriended Paul who also was a loner. His girlfriend, Lisa, had begun to also travel for work. She was a writer and could have done her job from anywhere and Paul just didn't understand her want and need to travel, at great expense, *his* great expense, for long periods.

Their friendship grew and as they began to share each other's life stories, passions, and secrets, their grief was also shared. Between Lisa's constant spending and lying about it to his face and Jack's blatant control over her, the abuse, and degradation.

Paul's breaking point was when Lisa returned home for mere hours only to turn back around and travel to Aruba for a new writing project. She explained to him, with the utmost confidence, that she would be spending her own money on simple expenses. While these simple expenses may have been true, she also stole cash Paul had stashed throughout the house and his credit cards, some of which she opened up in his name without him knowing. This, she spent on top-notch, well, everything. From alcohol to restaurants to strip clubs she spent every cent and lied directly to his face. The moment he brought it up to her, she denied it and even threatened to leave him. He simply couldn't take any more.

As Paul's troubles accumulated, so did Maggie's as she had been trying to convince Jack to start a family with her. Unfortunately, they were unsuccessful for the longest time. Naturally, this was all her fault. Jack had nothing to do with this. Each time she tested negatively, she received a beating from slaps and punches to belts and ropes. She couldn't take it anymore. Jack had already forced her to distance herself from her family, both physically and emotionally. Her friends all left her behind as he would get jealous and not allow her any pleasure or time with anyone but him. Maggie vented to Paul regularly, so much so that Paul felt a pull, an attraction, one that Maggie truly did not want. This got to Paul, he took this personally when Maggie would not act for herself.

Paul's plot began with simple degenerates; drug dealers, the homeless, whores. He worked out of his basement, essentially fashioning it into a dungeon. Since Lisa was rarely home, he simply added additional locks and changed out keys regularly to keep her out. At first, it was simple and to the point, beat and cause harm, taking out aggressions and acts of rage on these lowlifes. He would simply dump these poor souls in the nearby Ohio River in numerous locations, in far-off dumps, or even new construction sites which were just pouring foundations. Disposing of the bodies was easy enough as he could make long trips without anyone really paying notice. These murders were never truly tied together, at least not until Jack got involved.

As his horrific deeds increased in frequency, Paul's lust and need for more blood and death forced him to change their routine. He then targeted those who looked like both his and Maggie's emotionally lost lovers. These unfortunate doppelgangers helped Paul take out his anger and even left him emotionally level-headed and seemingly cured of his hatred for both of their partners. This only lasted about two or three victims when he realized his true need; to be emotionally attached in some fashion.

This began with lost loves, the first of whom broke Maggie's heart after a miscarriage. Paul heard all about this, in detail. His name was Alex. Alex was very unaware of the situation and when Paul drugged him Alex didn't even acknowledge her existence. This enraged Paul and he didn't even hesitate to take a butcher knife, cliche but his preferred method, and chopped off three of his fingers. This sparked something inside Paul, deep down. This was the start of his true serial killer mentality. After dispatching the fingers behind the nearby school, he watched the chaos ensue from the third-floor window.

Next victim: his stepfather, Frank. He would degrade Paul and send him to military school when he was young. This was a little more difficult for Paul to get near him. However, he creatively gathered intelligence where Frank would spend his evenings; in the Loose Moose Saloon. It was easy enough to slip some Rohypnol in his drink and even had the bartender help him get Frank to his SUV.

Paul's violence escalated as he removed Frank's left hand, the one which he beat Paul with regularly. Instead of simply leaving it somewhere for crowds to gawk, he had Frank sit at the window with them watching in sheer agony and hordes of people would circle the misplaced body part.

Instead of simply murdering and taking his rage out on those who had severely hurt both himself and Maggie in the past, he maimed and tortured them, leaving them suffering with a missing limb every other day. Each time he performed these macabre surgeries, Paul would stitch their wounds up to the best of his ability so this pain could be had all over again.

Paul would rotate his tortured victims between his and Maggie's past but unfortunately, their lives would expire after they were left as a torso with no extremities. He did dispose of these cadavers behind the hospital up the street and watched as municipal waste crews would dispose of them without notice.

Paul continued his spree with former family members and friends who left both of them high and dry. He felt like they were doing the world a favor, not to mention Maggie, and finally, after about a year, he grew tired of cleaning up both of their past lives. It was time to act and finish the job that made him truly begin this homicidal craze.

This all led to what he saw as his grand moment. The one he had been waiting all of his life for, disposing of both of their significant others with no remorse. However, after so long, Maggie finally found out she was pregnant and only told Paul, continuing his infatuation with her thinking he was her person and the closest thing to a family member he's ever had.

Even though Paul wanted to complete his mission, Maggie felt like something was off and even refused to see Paul any longer. One fatal evening, Jack took his frustrations out on Maggie, as he struggled to track down this serial killer. Paul, upon hearing this, had enough.

He knew it was time to complete his final and greatest feat, and finally, it would just be the two of them: Paul and Maggie. What he didn't realize is that Jack was close to solving these heinous crimes. This all came to a head that very day that Paul brought another package to Maggie's house, just another piece of evidence he had been planting all throughout this murder spree.

––––––––––––––––––––

Jack was forced to watch as his own wife removed the body parts of a woman he'd barely met but put in this position with his greed and pride. As he attempted to squirm away, call for help, and even fight back, Maggie kept him at bay. She continued to drug him and forced him to watch the incidents out the window and watched the news nightly as the story played on a near loop claiming that the Ohio River Killer had expanded his territory and spread fear throughout the entire country.

After she disclosed Paul's entire murderous rampage and cleared her conscience, she prepared to complete Paul's final grand design. As Jack's demise neared, she very slowly, slower than Paul's disgusting normalcy, began to take him apart piece by piece. She would extract pounds of flesh, simply leaving them on the road for stray dogs to devour. She deconstructed his limbs, leaving him with limited body parts. She began with his left hand, still wearing his wedding ring. This torture continued removing his right foot, the same which Lisa took from Paul. He pleaded with her for his life. He told her numerous times that she was an innocent victim who was wrapped up in this reign of terror

Maggie was irate. He acted as if he knew her but Jack was so far removed from their relationship that he didn't know anything about her anymore. He didn't even know that she was pregnant. She didn't want him to know.

He continued and asked her how many people she could help by showing them that she didn't harm anyone and that the truth was that Paul murdered all of these people. That she survived this brutality that she would be the center of attention and even get the spotlight put on her on the biggest stage.

Maggie did not want any attention, and Paul did that to her. He molded her, turning her into what she truly was: Paul's true love and the one to carry on his legacy.

Jack did not deserve to be part of Paul's story, she would create her own. She decided against following through with Paul's wishes, rather, Maggie took it upon herself to force Jack to suffer as long as possible.

After she loaded up her belongings, she planned on moving on. She wanted to go someplace else far away to raise her child, to 'help' others. So, without much more hesitation, she took the final piece of Jack: his hand, and his wedding band, and tossed them unceremoniously in that same dumpster that Paul and Lisa were placed inside of.

Maggie made an anonymous call to the police station from Paul's residence. She told them that Paul had done some terrible things and decided to end it all.

Her front-row seat to this extravaganza was her true send-off. She wanted to be there as the crowds formed, as the chaos ensued, and as the fear spread. She laid the severed hand, ring and all, outside the dumpster and allowed the blood to pour out. She waited in her SUV for her moment.

---

The anonymous call brought the police to Paul's basement, tying him to the Ohio River Killer once and for all. What they found when scouring the house was beyond comprehension. The mangled body of Jack was hung upside down in the basement, a gash on each cheek and forehead ultimately led to his body almost completely drained of blood. He was left to suffer to rot for crimes only known to one person who, to this day is still hard at work avenging those who need significant and specific help; righteous help.

# EVOLUTION: ARMAGEDDON

The air reeked of death. Decomposing bodies littered the streets outside of the safe house. A dark red mist rose from the carcasses as night fell once again. Jason sighed. *Only three?* He thought. *How can there only be three of us?* He urgently shook off the thought of self-pity.

"Make sure that door is sealed!" Jason yelled up from the basement.

Those beings broke in through the make-shift barrier earlier that day and they would surely return, especially come nightfall.

Jason limped up the cracked stairwell; a blood-soaked rag was tied around his leg. "You two hear me?" He grunted as he finally stepped up off the stairs onto the shattered remains of the kitchen.

"Yeah," a woman's voice echoed from the hall on the second story, "I'm trying to close off the hallway up here!"

Jason glanced through the wood panels out the window. The fallen beasts seemed to cover the ground like a sidewalk from their safe house to the road. At the moment, it appeared as though their small band of survivors had killed the remaining undead. Maybe the smell of living tissue guided them to Jason and his companions. "Good, just hurry up. Where's Dustin?" Jason leaned against the wall, trying to keep his weight off the injured leg.

The woman hustled down the stairs from the floor above. Her jet-black hair bobbed with her every step. "You need to stop worrying so much. We know how to survive. After all, it's been what, two months?"

A loud crash boomed from the back porch. Jason jumped from the wall, immediately pointing his Remington pump-action shotgun in that direction. "Dustin? Is that you?"

Ali placed a gentle hand on the weapon, "Of course it is." She stared into Jason's baby blue eyes. "He's doing a quick check around the house, remember?"

"Sorry. You know I get a little paranoid at night." He spun toward the basement entrance.

Without looking at Ali, he quietly corrected her, "And it's been nearly six months now." Her cheeks grew cherry red. It was hard keeping track of time, days, months, and (eventually) years. They had been without power since the backup generator gave way after a week of being hauled up in the grocery store. It was tough at first, making the changes necessary to survive. Eating little, sleeping only three or four hours a night, and regularly moving from town to town. They must have been in their twentieth safe house by now. Each move was for a different reason, even though most of the time it was because Jason was running out of his medicine.

Dustin shoved the mahogany bookshelf in front of the back door upon his return. "I see a few on the horizon, but nothing like earlier," his voice remained quite calm. "Everything else closed up?"

"Yeah, I finished upstairs, and we never messed with the front." She moved in close to Dustin, "Do you think he'll be alright? He's starting to act a little…"

"Scared?"

Ali scratched her head, "Yeah, I guess so. He's acting like he's never seen these things before. But he still keeps track of the days."

"I think that slash on his leg has him all shaken up." Dustin reached for the Browning pistol on the end table by the stairwell. "After all, he came *that* close to becoming one of those things."

Ali followed Dustin down the stairs. She slammed the basement door behind her and then ran a thin strand of fishing wire from the doorknob to the pin of the homemade explosive, which lay under the first step.

Jason collapsed on the couch out of pure exhaustion. He reached in his pack and pulled out a pill bottle. He removed two small, white pills and placed them gently in his mouth. Without even a swig of water, he swallowed them. "I've got about two days left here. We'll need to move soon."

"We're running out of food too." Dustin tossed an empty can on the floor. "We should move tomorrow."

"As long as they don't swarm like they did this morning," Jason reminded him.

Ali reached the bottom of the flight of stairs. She reached on her back, unhinged the rusting rifle, and chucked it toward the couch. "I need a new one." She smirked. "This thing is going to kill me yet."

"Hey, that's a classic." Dustin smiled back. We'll get an early start and find a safe-house and make a supply run tomorrow."

Jason snored from the couch.

"I guess he'll take the first turn tonight." Ali walked over to Jason's pack. She reached inside and grabbed the pill bottle. "What are these? Antibiotics? Or something better?" she asked with a smirk.

Jason snatched the pill bottle from her grasp without a sound. "None of your damn business, Teach." That was what he called Ali from the time they met. After all, they met during a one-sided firefight against an enormous horde of oncoming undead. He never caught her name until a few hours later. She had a name tag on. One that you would see a teacher wear. This particular one read 'Hi, I'm Mrs. Newhouse.' That was the fateful day she lost her son to those creatures.

"Wow. For an old Marine, you still have those skills, don't you?" Dustin slumped beside him. He reached in his pocket and pulled out a pack of cigarettes. There was one left. "Well, I found something else we need."

The groaning began like any other gathering of the 'Burst' victims. They echoed from outside, most likely from a large group of them. But they stopped. The groans, the footsteps, everything.

"What are they doing?" Ali asked no one in particular, reaching for her rifle.

Jason jumped to attention. His shotgun aimed toward the door before his legs were securely under him. "Shh." Dustin pointed the Browning in the same direction. He reached into his pack and grabbed a few clips. He tossed them in his pocket.

A long, drawn-out rumble ricocheted from the outside. The ground shook. Books from the bookcase upstairs flew from their places while the remaining glass in the windows collapsed out of their seals.

"What the hell?" Dustin jumped back.

"That's why they stopped," Jason pointed a single finger toward the basement door. As far as he was concerned, they needed to defend themselves from whatever was charging at them. There was no other way out. This was it. No turning back.

The basement door flew inward as the gigantic beast slammed into it. It tumbled down the steps, pulling the grenade with it. This wasn't an ordinary undead abomination.

The "normal" undead ones were exactly that; not living but not dead. They all smelled of decaying tissue. They all had some sort of battle scar, whether it was a large gash across the stomach, a chunk out of their neck, or a missing limb. There was always some way to tell how they became one of them; one of the infected.

This one, however, was different. It no longer even resembled a human being like the others. Its knees were bent in the opposite direction, almost like a dog's leg. The creature's arms stretched out as long as its legs. The thing's elbows protruded out of the skin, capable of acting as razor-sharp weapons. Its head transformed in a way that connected the neck to the rear of its head, resembling the head of a shark. The creature's fingertips had been gnawed back until the flesh revealed pale white bones.

It lay stunned at the bottom of the steps. A loud grunt sounded from its nostrils as it came to. The mutant pulled itself upwards on its two hind legs. The colossal creature, which stood over eight feet tall, paused momentarily.

"Dustin," Jason whispered. "Back up."

The creature lurched forward toward Dustin with an outstretched, inhuman arm. A growl stunned the already petrified Dustin.

Ali pulled the trigger of her hand-me-down rifle. The bullet struck the beast in the shoulder. It only irritated the thing. Without turning its attention from its future meal, the brute charged without warning. Jason fired the pump-action shotgun twice. He thrust hot lead into the creature's rotten flesh.

Only slightly thrown off balance, the rank monster threw its protracted arm into Dustin's paralyzed body. He crashed against the stone wall below the staircase. His arm twisted around behind his back. Blood poured from the fractured limb.

Ali unloaded her clip into the beast's head, tearing holes through its skull. Black liquid discharged from the wounds, still unimpaired, the creature stomped forward. Its sight was set on its next victim.

"Jason!" Ali stepped back.

Jason had already taken this advice. His back was against the farthest wall from the giant. His shotgun was already smoking as he drained it once more. It was ready to pump more lead into the thing's back. "Get out the way, Teach!"

Ali ducked out of the way of the creature's swing. She turned away but slipped on Dustin's gun which had slid under her.

Another three rounds. Four rounds, now, were shot into the beast's midsection. Black goo dripped profusely from its head and what should be its abdomen. The wounds did not slow it.

As Ali stumbled to find her balance, a large, cold hand dug its fleshless nails into her shoulder. She let out an ear-piercing shriek as the thing squeezed tight. In the creature's deadly grasp, Ali could feel herself being raised off the ground a good three feet. Blood soaked from her open wound to her toes.

Jason continued to pour shotgun lead into the creature's side. Still no effect. It opened its mouth wide to let out a long, mindless groan. It bent its head low and took a chunk of flesh out of Ali's opposite shoulder with its razor-sharp teeth, spewing blood over itself.

Behind the monster, Dustin rolled over. His arm was barely attached to his shoulder as he lay in a pool of his own blood. He glanced at the creature, still holding Ali in its strong claw. Looking down, Dustin noticed his pistol under the creature; obviously out of reach.

The normally infected monstrosities climbed over one another at the top of the stairs. Jason saw them out of the corner of his eye and knew they were in serious trouble. This mutated creature must be the leader of this pack. He theorized that the 'Blast' was some sort of terrorist attack. If that was truly the case, there was no way the deadly chemicals would only create mindless cannibals. No, there were intelligences to them. There were leaders. The chemicals only altered human DNA. The different strains of this disease would eventually lead to some mutations. This was one of those unusual mutations. It must have been a leader. The normals gathered outside and waited for it to make its move.

Jason placed a perfectly accurate shot over the monster's shoulder but hit a more human-looking undead directly in the knee, destroying what was left of the muscle and bone holding it in place. It was launched down the staircase.

The undead toppled down the stairs and landed beside Dustin. Even before it landed, Dustin began pounding away on it. He threw punches with his one good arm and kicked rapidly. More of those things crept down the basement, surrounding Dustin. He knew there was only one thing to do. He reached out, holding the creature off with his feet. He grabbed hold of the small metal device still attached to the fishing line.

Ali's face had turned almost a light bluish color. The brute thrashed her about, draining the blood from her slender body. Her eyes were shut, more than likely passing out from the blood loss.

Another shotgun blast surged throughout the basement with a deafening ring, bouncing off the thick concrete walls. Jason picked off another undead behind the beast flailing Ali. He detected Dustin's movement and panicked. "No! Dustin don't d –"

An enormous explosion threw the crowd of lifeless beings in every direction. They scattered up the stairs, toward the monster. The blast was so strong that it even threw some of the undead over it, nearly capsizing Jason. The blast had severed the large creature's dog-like legs. It released Ali and let out a growl; not of pain but anger. It clawed its way toward Jason. The black ooze still seeped from its abrasions, leaving a trail from Ali.

More shotgun smoke filled the air around Jason after he placed a few well-aimed buck shots in the monster's eyes. He blinded the thing, even though it still thrashed on the charred cement floor. He tightened the blood-soaked rag around his leg then shuffled over to Ali.

She passed out, too much blood was lost. Jason turned back to the amputated creature; he shot three shells out of his shotgun then shoved

121

the burning hot barrel on Ali's wounds. He was able to close the wounds surprisingly quickly. The now black and dark-red openings puffed up and seeped an ooze of sorts.

Jason tossed her over his shoulder, wincing at the pain shooting up his leg. He picked up her rifle and slung it over his shoulder. He tossed Dustin's pistol in his pocket then reached for a red can sitting under the desk behind the monster. He gave one last glance at Dustin's bloody, dismembered body. "Goodbye old friend. I'm sure I'll see you soon."

Trails of gasoline lead from the monster to the back entrance, once guarded by a bookshelf. Jason shot his last slug out of the shotgun at the puddle of gasoline. Sparks shot off the ground as the liquid shot up in flames. The trail quickly followed the spark as the walls of their safe house caught fire. The monster underground moaned and howled as it burned to its final death.

"Time to move, Teach." Jason tossed his shotgun in his backpack next to Ali and turned toward the desolate road, only lit by the jumping flames behind him.

---

The sunrise was beautiful. Ali opened her eyes at the perfect time. She sat up and stretched her arms out. "What was that thing?" She rolled out of the makeshift tent inside some sort of sporting goods store.

"Some sort of mutation?" Jason had already been up searching for supplies but stayed close enough to Ali to see her. He was afraid a bite from that thing would have changed her faster than normal. To this point, though, there were no signs. "How are you feeling?" He limped back to the tent, the shotgun in hand.

"Been better," she smiled up toward him. She stood using the rifle as a crutch. "Thank you." A long pause ensued. "You could have left me back there to…to change."

Jason smiled, "I wanted to make sure I had a chance to say goodbye." He reached for his pack. "I'm sorry about Dustin." He gulped hard, unsure how she would take his brutal death.

"What happened to him?" She bowed her head.

"He sacrificed himself for us." Jason reached for the pistol tucked in his worn jeans. "He killed them all with the explosive."

Without much more reaction Ali grabbed her pack and joined him. "You ready?"

"Yeah, let's get moving. I'd like to find a pharmacy around here to find more meds. Speaking of which," Jason reached in his pack and grabbed two more pills. Once more he downed them with a quick gulp.

"I mean sure, okay, but I mean…" She shrugged. "Are you ready to do what's necessary? You know, when it's time."

Jason lowered his head. "Of course. I'll make it quick."

"Speaking of those pills…" Ali smirked.

"They're not like that. They're my Synthroid." Jason began their long hike to the next small town. His limp still affected him, "It's for my removed Thyroid. I had cancer when I was seven years old."

"So, you're medicine dependent? That's why we need to keep moving. To replenish your pills." Ali reached for her burning shoulder and let out a slight groan.

"That and so we can reach the quarantined area. Supposedly up north around New England."

Jason pulled out a map. "It looks like we should follow this interstate until we reach Trenton then pick up I-87 North."

Ali didn't bother looking at the map, she was just along for the company now. "Sounds like a plan. Should we grab a car this time?" During their last big move, the interstate was too crowded with cars so they never even bothered getting in one.

"As long as it's open. And we can find one with gas." He folded the map back and stuffed it in the worn backpack.

---

Most cars had been depleted of gas from someone driving it then ditching it. Others had been filtered of gas by survivors. Some cars had been tipped over or destroyed by packs of the undead. This time, luckily, the two of them found a semi-open lane and a nice, near-perfect BMW.

The ride was quiet as they took turns. Jason felt comfortable sleeping, even though he knew Ali was going to change. She did not show any signs, not yet.

It was a long and quiet drive. How did he get here?

His mind wandered…to his wife…

She was a slow turn. From what Jason remembered, the turn simply started with a cold sweat, nothing major. After a day or so, her skin turned a greenish hue as though it began the decomposition process. Her veins puffed out to the surface of her already thin skin. Her eyes turned a cherry red then, very quickly, altered to a dark-gray color. At that point, she still acted like herself, just in excessive pain and was extremely uncomfortable. Her eyesight blurred followed by her speech slurring.

After she was bit by their son, Jason simply tried to keep her as comfortable as possible. He kept her warm. He fed her and stayed with her. He witnessed the transformation; it was the most painful thing he ever witnessed. He knew what he had to do but he couldn't. He killed their son, their one and only son, but he couldn't kill his love. Jason tied her down to the bed, crying the entire time. He kissed her goodbye. His last memory of her was of him speeding off in their minivan, leaving her behind for fate to figure out.

During that seemingly endless drive, alone in the minivan, Jason heard a broadcast on the emergency frequency. Supposedly there was a haven just east of New York, around the Connecticut area. According to this crackling announcement, the 'Blast' hadn't spread that far and, as of the time of the broadcast, the undead did not spread their diseases to anyone past that quarantine zone.

Jason's minivan ran out of gas near Raleigh. He took to walking. Aside from burning cars and blowing newspapers, the streets were deserted. No humans – or dead – anywhere in sight. Hunger overtook him. He made his way to a Food Lion on Western Boulevard. Jason stuffed his face with anything edible, which was practically everything but the building. At that point, it had been almost a full day since he last ate.

This was the moment Jason had met Dustin. Naturally, Dustin saved his life. From what he could remember, Dustin was hauled up in the break room with two other survivors. The three of them must have heard Jason scrounging around in the store. Just as they exited the break room to investigate, a pack of diseased creatures smashed through the front glass just behind Jason.

They moved fast. Faster than anyone could have imagined, based on pop culture at least. They weren't the stereotypical cliche Romero zombie; slow and brainless. They weren't necessarily intelligent but also not stupid. If they had the capabilities, as in all of their limbs, they could move fast.

The three survivors darted toward Jason, pulling him back. Dustin smashed one of the undead in the temple with a fire extinguisher. It fell back, losing its balance.

One of the other survivors broke a wooden mop over the back of another creature. This one didn't even falter. With no other option, this man stepped back in awe.

Without a word, the four men scampered back to the break room. They slammed the door and began to desperately search the room for another exit. They came across an air duct, just large enough for the grown men to fit in. When they made it to the roof, the group peered over the edge of the building. Their eyes grew wide as they witnessed the horror awaiting them. There had to be nearly two hundred undead circling the building.

They jumped about fifteen feet down from the roof, landing on top of cars parked in the lot. They jumped from one to another until they reached Dustin's truck. At that point, Dustin and one of his comrades vaulted in the cab. Jason and the other survivors sat in the bed. As they pulled away, Jason and this new found friend fended the creatures off from climbing up onto the truck.

They headed north toward Washington, D.C.

---

Jason was snapped back to reality as Ali announced, "We're here.". Her voice appeared to be getting weaker. "Trenton, New Jersey. Should we get your pills?"

Jason was still a little groggy but was ready to go at a moment's notice. He reached for the shotgun, then pulled up Dustin's pistol from the floor. "Yeah, let's find a pharmacy. We should get gas too."

The pair slowly drove down the street, keeping an ever-vigilant eye for any lurking monsters. The night was soon to fall. They needed to find a safe house. Jason knew that he needed Ali's help before she…changed.

After about fifteen minutes into their search, and only about thirty minutes to go before nightfall, they came across a large CVS along Olden Avenue.

"Okay, let's hurry in there." Jason jumped out of the classy car. "We should hole up here for the night."

Ali followed his lead and ran toward the previously vandalized pharmacy. She followed him through a broken pane of glass into the dark store. "Should we get back there?" She pointed toward the manager's office sign guiding them to the rear of the store.

Jason thought for a moment. "Yeah, why not? Go ahead and check it out. I'll grab my Synthroid before it gets too dark."

Without a moment's hesitation, Ali shuffled to the back room. She pulled her rifle from her shoulder and was ready. "Grab me some pain killers, would you?" She gruffly whispered. He didn't answer but did reach for a large bottle of Advil. He pocketed it but moved toward the pharmacy in the opposite corner. He knew full well he was going to look for something a little stronger for her, but just in case.

When he reached the pharmacy, he noticed dried blood streaks that lead from the counter, down an aisle of acne medications. Jason's shotgun was aimed and ready for anything and everything. Out of the corner of his eye, he noticed something shuffling across from him. He spun; the shotgun still aimed.
"Hurry up!" Ali shouted from the manager's office. "It's clear!"

*I must be seeing things now!* Jason told himself. He shook off that thought but as he turned to double check a sole creature leaped on top of him. The beast's tongue was waving in the air, aiming for his face. Black slime dripped from the oversized muscle. The goo splashed on his arm, eating away at his flesh. His arm instinctively flinched and allowed the being's hungry mouth all the closer to his neck.

One-shot rang out. The mutated undead was forced from him and crashed against the pharmacy counter. The rifle smoked next to him from Ali's rifle.

"You don't know how to ask for help, do you?" A smirk grew from cheek to cheek. "Come on," she offered her hand. "The sun's going down."

Jason was still in shock as he was pulled up from the tiled floor. He wiped his arm clean from the ooze that dripped from the beast's tongue. "Another mutated one."

"Why? After six months of nothing but the…uhh. normal ones, why are they everywhere now?" Ali asked, her voice cracking.

Jason shook his head and ducked behind the counter. He reached toward the shelf holding his medicine. He unzipped his pack and held it open under the shelf. "I'll sort them later. Let's get to the office"

They spent the entire night without incident. They sped off as soon as the sun rose over Trenton. This time Jason drove. He needed to keep an eye on Ali at this point. During the night, she began sweating. She grew cold. The next step was the change of her skin color.

---

His mind wondered again as he drove down the emptied highway…

Nearly five months ago, when Jason's group of four survivors reached the capital, the entire area had been severely ravaged. None of them believed a single soul could have survived an undead attack like that. Cars had been overturned, some set on fire. Papers flew around in the dry air. Bodies were scattered across the streets. Some wore army apparel. Some were children.

The group heard one echoing shriek; a woman. It sounded like it came from the elementary school nearly a hundred yards away. The school was half demolished. Holes were blown in the brick siding, likely from the soldiers using their heavy weapons.

They pulled up in their truck to a large, gaping hole in the side of the school to find a woman. She was still wearing her name tag: 'Hi, I'm Mrs. Newhouse.' A teacher? She was cradling a child in her arms; he was bitten near his ankle. Blood still poured from the injury. She was surrounded. There were twenty infected closing in on her.

The men dismounted the truck and groped for any weapons they could find. Jason grabbed a shotgun from a fallen soldier. Dustin pulled a pistol out from the same army-man's holster. The two other survivors grabbed a pair of chairs that were strewn across the classroom.

Jason jumped in first and blasted away at two of them with the pump-action shotgun. Their blood spewed over the woman and the child. Dustin placed perfect shots in five living dead, emptying his clip. The other two swung the chairs wildly at the pack of them. They knocked ten of them away from the woman. One of these survivors was overtaken and torn to bits. Jason pumped the shotgun and unloaded five more slugs into the walking dead; blowing them to pieces.

The three remaining men helped the woman and the child into the bed of the truck. During the ride away from the carnage, the child's skin began to change color. Jason knew that this child was changing. They found an abandoned hotel that night.

As the sun rose, the group was astonished to find the child squirming and writhing in pain on a bed in the next room. Jason had convinced this woman, who was unceremoniously introduced to the group as Ali, to keep this boy there for the night. During that long night, the group was told that this boy Ali had been protecting was no student, he was her son, Drew. As they loaded up their truck, Drew stopped breathing. Ali was in shambles and rocked him as if he would wake up…he did.

The now undead Drew thrashed about and jumped to its feet. With a limp, it charged at Dustin's remaining friend and tore open a large gash in his stomach. The disease instantly shocked his system and spread into his bloodstream.

The creature turned toward Ali and just as it was in an arm's reach, Jason fired the reloaded shotgun. The smoke cleared. Drew's body lay finally dead on the floor.

Ali was in tears as the trio pulled away, only to find that the truck's tank was empty. They could not find any gasoline so they took to foot. They hastily grabbed supplies and found safe houses along their way. Their goal was Baltimore where a military base was supposed to be quarantined.

It wasn't.

---

Jason snapped out of his daydreams. They reached the Connecticut border with a greeting sign that read 'Connecticut Welcomes You.' Hopefully, they would find their safe haven there. Thank God, no undead.

"Teach, we're –" His stomach dropped. Ali's skin was a bluish tint. Her veins puffed outward through her skin. Her eyes, black as the pistol he reached for. "Ali." He shook her. "Ali, we're here. It's Connecticut."

She rolled over. "Drew…Drew, is that you?" Her voice is calm but unsettling.

"Yeah," a tear rolled down Jason's cheek. "It's me." He raised Dustin's pistol to her temple. "I'm sorry."

A loud boom echoed from the BMW. Brain matter sprayed across the window. Jason reached for the door handle and pulled hard. The door popped open and Jason shoved her out of the opening of the car.

He stepped on the gas. Now, more than ever, Jason wanted nothing more than to get the hell out of there. He drove and drove and drove. "Where the hell is the safe zone?" He slammed the steering wheel.

Finally, a sign appeared: 'Hartford 5 Miles Left Lane Only.'

"*This must be it,*" he thought. "Hartford, the safe haven of Hartford." He let out a long sigh of relief.

---

The Blast occurred suddenly, without warning. Jason had a perfect view of it. The bomb, or whatever it was, blew up only twenty miles from his home in Columbia, South Carolina. The news said the nuke never actually went off. Eventually, they admitted it wasn't a bomb meant to blow up. It was meant to distribute biochemical weapons.

All that he could see out of his window was a bright light that shot out like a bullet. The sheer force of the light knocked him backward. Little did he know that he, and everyone in the eastern United States, was just contaminated with a chemical called Velodrome.

Initially, Velodrome was a chemical used to reduce the size of cancerous sores. After months of testing, it was shown to have horrific effects on the human body. None of the patients ever died but their blood cells began dying and spread to their skin, killing it over time. They decomposed while still alive. Before anyone knew exactly what this chemical truly was or the potential it could be used for, Korean spies stole the chemical and began experimenting with it. They found that if the effects could be increased, they could reanimate the dead cells.

The "V-Bomb," as it was nicknamed, was never assessed. However, it was sold to China before it was deactivated. After the 'Blast,' no one knew where it had come from nor how to stop it. The only thing that was known was if anyone with an open wound came into contact with Velodrome, their cell count would significantly drop. Ultimately, their bodies would begin to shut down.
After a day or so of being infected, the victim would finally die, however, they would come to life. This occurred after a mere hour of their hearts stopping. When they came back to life, they would not have a pulse nor a heartbeat. Their brain functions would slow dramatically, shutting off most intelligence and all memories. All they knew was survival - survival by eating human tissue.

Only months after the 'Blast' spread across the eastern seaboard, the chemical began to evolve, expand, and transform the infected into something more. Something unstoppable, something that only knew human destruction.

Jason finally arrived. The thick concrete wall stood at least twelve feet tall. It was outfitted with strands of barbed wire above it. No one would get past that. Every few hundred feet stood an overlooking guard post housing two soldiers, each controlled their own mounted machine gun.

There was a single doorway with a decontamination room attached to it. There were no lines of survivors waiting to get in. But there *were* soldiers that lined the doorway. Each soldier wore a white hazardous material jumpsuit and carried an M-60 machine gun. This was easily capable of mowing down dozens of undead oppositions in just seconds.

Jason pulled around to the entrance and waited for some semblance of instruction. His spirits were raised, there was hope. If only Ali were here. If only Dustin were here. If only….

He looked out the opposite side of the car. "Ali?" Jason threw open the dented door of the BMW. *She must have followed me!* He thought as he jumped out of the car. "Help!" he motioned to the soldiers. "That's my friend! Help her!"

Jason ran up to the soldiers, "Please! Please!"

The soldier grabbed his arm and pulled him toward the entrance. "There is nothing we can do." He said very calmly as if it were rehearsed. "Please, enter the decontamination zone."

Jason pulled away only to stare in horror as his friend grotesquely transformed. Ali, or what was left of her, pulled her arms out from her sides. A thin piece of skin had grown between her spine and each of her arms. She began flapping her arms and ran hastily. Suddenly, she took flight. As she approached him, Jason could see how the disease changed her.

She had evolved. Her head mutated and stretched outward, as if she grew a beak of sorts. Ali's teeth protruded both up and down outside of his newly formed beak.

One of the soldiers ran out toward Jason and opened fire on the creature. The creature swooped, quite gracefully for an undead monster, and grabbed the soldier with its sharp teeth and lashed out at Jason with an elongated tongue. Blood discharged from the laceration made by the razor-sharp teeth and Jason's arm immediately began to burn.
As the monstrosity turned up toward the sky, the army opened fire. It fell violently back toward Earth. An inhumane thud accompanied a blood curdling shriek as the creature hit the soil.

"Ali…" he murmured. Tears again trickled down his cheeks. He was hauled back to the entrance by two soldiers. He didn't fight them. He knew he had to get to safety.

---

Jason was stripped down to his gray boxers. Multiple guns were pointed at him from every angle. A long and frigid air blew all over his body. This was followed by a burst of what could best be described as cold as water but as putrid smelly as vomit. They yanked him out of the plastic chamber, and he slammed to the ground.

Jason hunched his back and fell onto his knees. His eyes began to itch. His skin began to burn. He reached for his arm; it still blistered from that creature's tongue. He raised his head, "No," he murmured.

"Look…his eyes…" The closest soldier to him shouted.

"He's infected!" The soldiers circled him. "Open fire!"

---

"Sir," the soldier stood erect. "The reanimated have taken to the sky. We just shot one down."

An older man behind a desk stood, limped over to a monitor. "I knew this would happen. They are evolving. They will all be changing soon. We need to prepare the forces. Build up the exterior wall. Assign more scouts to the towers."

"Yes sir," the soldier saluted him.
"And would you please prepare that nuke? We need to launch it by nightfall." He sat back down in his leather chair.

"What about survivors?" The soldier asked as concern radiated from his shaky tone.

"These things will not stop. We need to destroy everything…and everyone if necessary."

# TALE OF TWO LOVES

He was fueled by hatred. His blood boiled. He trudged up the muddy hillside, the rain blinded him. The bag draped over his shoulder weighed him down like a ton of bricks. As Rocky struggled toward the dilapidated brick building, he couldn't help but urge himself on. Pushing through the throbbing warmth of worn-out muscles.

"She would want this," he whispered to himself. "This is where she wants to be."

---

His life was over. He lost his house, his friends, his job. Lucy immediately kicked him out. All of his clothing, toiletries, and personal belongings were strewn about her yard. His rage pulsed, but he never raised his voice. He simply gathered his things and organized his car to accommodate his suddenly chaotic life.

Lucy thought her friends and family could talk some sense into him, he was wrong. Not only did he lose her, but every single one of his friends took Lucy's side. He called her mother in tears. She promised to speak with her daughter and figure everything out. The next thing he knew, Rocky received a restraining order to stay away from Lucy and her entire family.

His manager at his lowly coffee shop job was close friends with Lucy's father. Suffice it to say, Rocky's minimum wage job did not last another day. He was simultaneously informed that he was to be under a police investigation for stealing cash out of the register.

Rocky gave up everything for Lucy. His career was flushed down the toilet when Rocky followed her to the outskirts of Pittsburgh. The move from North Carolina was stressful enough, but when Lucy forced him to take on a barista job at a local Starbucks, any confidence he may have been destroyed. There was nothing for him in Pittsburgh. Back in Kitty Hawk, Rocky was a historian. His vast knowledge of the Wright brothers and the first plane seemed endless. In Pittsburgh, he could name over 20 flavors of coffee, oh what an accomplishment.

Every close friend back home warned him that she was bad news. When he moved north with Lucy, he cut ties with nearly every single one of them. Lucy's friends became his friends. When she kicked him out, Rocky had no one to talk to or to vent to or to help him or keep him sane.

His parents passed away in a brutal murder-suicide just two months earlier. Lucy wouldn't allow him to attend the funeral. She claimed that her beliefs prevented her from doing so. In her eyes, a suicide would not allow one to get buried. In her eyes, it was forbidden. In her eyes, it was a sin.

When it was all said and done, Rocky was alone. His only family, his only friend, his only purpose was Lucy.

---

Finally, as he crested the hillside, Rocky's sweaty hands released the bag. It was nearly eaten by the Earth under his feet. He kept a single hand around the strap, ensuring it would not sink in the quicksand-like mud.

Rocky knocked twice at the medieval, rustic door.

It flew open. Dim candle light flickered as a dark shadow backed away from the entrance. Red eyes and yellow teeth greeted him. The figure backed away and pointed down the hall, "This way, they're ready." Rocky reached back down for the bag, slung it over his shoulder, and continued inside behind the acquaintance.

He struggled to keep up in the dark hallway. Shadows jumped and danced all around him. It felt as though he were being greeted by a party. One in which he had not felt since he moved to the small industrial city.

His partner seemed to run, fly even, down the darkened hall. Rocky tried to keep up but could only follow the wretched scent. He began to second guess this. Did he make the right choice? It was too late at this point to turn back now.

Finally, after what felt like an eternity of darkness, a bright white light led him to the end of the path. The weight of the bag already felt like it was lifted. A new day was about to dawn.

---

Only a year in Pittsburgh was plenty for Lucy to second guess the decision to uproot. Her original passion for teaching, which drew her so far north, had worn thin. She spent much of her life working overtime to try to support her lowly boyfriend. He vowed to help out, do whatever he could to support her dream. He took the first opportunity he saw, utilizing her father's connections to a Starbucks manager. A minimum wage barista; oh, what a life they could afford.

She tutored kids and taught adult classes more often than not. Her weekends were booked up working with inner-city kids and their extracurricular projects. This left barely any time for their love life or any kind of life.

Rocky was lazy, unmotivated, and had no career aspirations. What else could she do? Lucy found out that he was stealing from work, from her father's close friend nonetheless. There was no longer a connection, no spark.

She originally thought that getting away from their families and on their own would bring them closer. All the responsibility and busy schedules pulled them even further from one another. She tried to push Rocky to see a counselor with her. She tried to introduce him to her work friend's significant others. Nothing worked. The space between them just grew larger and larger.

When Rocky's parents passed away, Lucy begged him to attend the funeral. She claimed that he needed to be there for his family and support his younger siblings. He refused to go home. He claimed that he could not return to such a depressing funeral. He didn't think they deserved to be buried. Lucy wanted to attend with him. To no avail, he just used his job as an excuse.

Lucy's passion became a job. She stopped enjoying it. The stress built up to the point that she needed out. She tried everything to soothe her mind, but when it came down to it; there was no easy way out.

She tried to talk to him. His anger reigned supreme.

The room was so bright. It felt like the first glimpse of a sunset after a long night of pure darkness. Rocky dropped the large bag in front of the robed man. The sweat had begun to pour out from his forehead. He wiped it with his rolled-up sweatshirt sleeve.

Rocky knelt beside the bag. A dark liquid already built up around it, leaving an outline. Just the rain and mud, he was sure of it. He started to unzip it. "No," a low, booming voice echoed. "I will continue building our masterpiece."

Rocky backed away from the bag. He looked down to his feet like a small child being scolded. He put his hands in his pockets and simply nodded.

The robed figure pointed back to the door. "You must return."

Rocky inched back toward the door, anxious to leave. He grabbed the keys from his pocket and threw his hood back over his head, oddly resembling his counterpart.

"One more piece to the puzzle and our work here will be done." The thing effortlessly picked up the bag and awaited Rocky's exit. "She will be proud," it boomed.

---

That fateful day that changed their lives forever came as a shock to Rocky, literally and figuratively.

He got home from his day shift around 3 PM. Lucy was surprisingly home before him.

All Monsters are Human

Rocky always went straight to the shower after work to wash off any coffee smell. His first stop was the bedroom.

Lucy was sitting quietly at the foot of the bed. Her look was cold, almost dead. Rocky sat next to her and brushed her hair behind her ear, as he would do from time to time. He gingerly asked if everything was okay. But her silence was more than enough to worry him.

She glanced up at him and said simply, "we're done."

Rocky withdrew, his eyes blurred and his head immediately ached. He sobbed endlessly, unable to get much of a word out.

Lucy's suitcase was already packed and laid next to her on the bed. She explained that Rocky was the cause for all of her pain, stress, and agony. She showed no emotion. She was to stay with her mother for a week or so to clear her head.

Rocky was still silent. He could have lashed out. He could have thrown her suitcase against the door. He could have thrown her against the door. He could have thrown the chair across the kitchen. He could have thrown her across the kitchen. He could have punched a hole in the wall. He could have punched her.

But he didn't.

He didn't do anything.

Lucy left without much more of a peep or tear from Rocky. But the anger built.

The drive back to their house in the torrential downpour was much easier than he imagined. Rocky was enthusiastic to finish this new job. He was excited and happy for the first time since their move to Pittsburgh.

The headlights glared through the raindrops, but he didn't stop. The engine roared as his old Chevy Beretta hit 100 miles an hour. The winding backroads, typically on the verge of flooding, did not bother him. His grip on the wheel was that of a skilled wheelman. The drive that normally lasts 45 minutes was cut to an unimaginable 15-minute speedway.

Rocky rushed into the house after sending the car to a screeching halt.

After fifteen minutes of some rustling around inside, a hooded Rocky strolled buoyantly back to the car with another bag slung over his shoulder. A smirk peered out from under his hood and a soft tune of "Whistle While You Work" could be heard through his puckered lips.

There was no rush on his way back down the road. The rain lightened up, so the drive should have been slightly easier. But this time, Rocky's venture back felt more like a Sunday afternoon stroll with no urgency or speed. Even with the rain, Rocky rolled his window and continued whistling his merry tune.

As he pulled up to the parking space next to the decrepit brick and mortar structure, Rocky's headlights reflected off a rusted-out sign labeled "Welcome to Dixmont Asylum."

She had to do it. Lucy had been getting anxiety attacks and was sick for days on end. She tried everything she could think of, this was the last resort. She tried to prepare herself for the worst. Lucy knew about Rocky's anger issues. She fears that he would take her suggestion the wrong way and hurt himself, or her.

Lucy was off for the summer, so she stayed home to pack up a suitcase and waited for Rocky to get home from work. She had made arrangements to stay with her mother for a week, just to get her head back on straight and figure things out. After all, these problems don't just fall on one person in a relationship.

She tried to stay calm and talk through it with Rocky, explaining her stance and reasoning, but he would not hear any of it. Lucy tried to run, get out, and away from him as quickly as possible.

His anger got the best of him as it had in the past. Rocky grabbed her suitcase out of her clutched grasp and thrashed it against the wall. Her belongings scattered all over. She ran through the doorway just as Rocky grabbed the rocking chair. He whipped it through the doorway. As she stood just inside the front door, Rocky grabbed Lucy by the neck. He slammed her against the foyer wall.

When she awoke, Rocky was gone. Lucy sped to her mother's house and did not look back. Her week-long experiment changed their lives forever.

---

Rocky trudged up the hillside one last time. Once again, he banged twice on the old door. His hooded companion directed him down the same corridor, to the same bright room. This time, Rocky was welcomed to sit and stay.

The robe-clad being directed Rocky with an outstretched hand towards a long, metallic table laid against the back of the room. Based upon the crude design, it was most likely an old-fashioned operating table used in the golden age of the asylum.

Candles lit a path to the table. Rocky sauntered over slowly as a chair was already pulled out and waited for him to take a seat. The table was set to accommodate four people. Four plates, four bowls, four sets of silverware, and four chairs were set out. Two of those chairs were currently occupied.

Rocky didn't think much of it. It was going to be a party, he might as well make the best of it and introduce himself. He took his seat and leaned in to introduce himself to the two other guests.

To his surprise, the other company had black bags draped over their heads. He still gave the formal cordials. All he received were some gags and moans. His only thought was, "Very rude."

Rocky glanced around, slightly hungry now. His host, who he figured was the fourth guest, was nowhere to be seen.

---

Rocky gave Lucy her space. He thought he was doing the right thing. He felt a little more comfortable after speaking with Lucy's mother as soon as possible. She claimed she would speak with Lucy and try to help them through this tough time.

After about a week or so, Rocky was shocked to receive a restraining order from both Lucy and her mother, who he trusted. He didn't think much of it. He continued his job search and kept up with the house just like Lucy expected of him.

Another week passed and he grew impatient. The restraining order was just a piece of paper, right? Rocky loved her. That's all that mattered. He packed a black overnight bag filled with clothes, old cards, pictures, stuffed animals; anything that would remind Lucy of Rocky.

Once he arrived at her parents' house, Rocky quickly made his way to the door with the bag over his shoulder. His disappointment and frustration grew when her parents explained that she was actually on her way to their house to collect some of her belongings.

They reiterated the importance of a restraining order and that they will not hesitate to call the cops. Rocky was taken aback. Her parents, whom he adored, threatened him.

With nowhere else to turn, Rocky headed back home in hopes of running into Lucy. He sped as fast as he could. It still felt like it took the entire evening to return home. By the time he pulled into the driveway, the sun had already set, and there was no sign of Lucy.

However, there was a crudely written note left on the kitchen table. It was an invitation to the old asylum down on Route 65: Dixmont. He was asked to attend a small gathering that very night, hosted by "Me."

---

Her peace didn't last long. Lucy claimed a restraining order immediately after Rocky's flip out and beating. She stayed with her parents until they could get her life sorted out. For the next couple of days after the abuse, Lucy was given police escorts around the hospital.

Rocky must not have understood the severity of the situation though; he continuously called, texted, and emailed her. It was apology after apology one day, and the next day everything was Lucy's fault.
She had come to the conclusion that he just flipped.

When the cops stormed their house to look for Rocky, he was nowhere to be found. In fact, the house looked like it had been abandoned since Lucy left.

'Where was Rocky?' That was her ever-lingering question in the back of her mind. Lucy was scared; not only for herself but for her family and friends.

Apparently, Rocky had also been in contact with their friends. He was threatening those who did not agree with him – which was all of them. Even Rocky's brother called Lucy to make sure she was okay.

Where was Rocky?

Her question was answered about a month after his attack. He showed up at her front door.

Luckily – or not so lucky – Lucy's parents spotted him sauntering up to their short driveway. They forced her into the crawl space in the basement until he left. All she could do was wait him out.

He was cordial and polite, he simply asked to speak with Lucy. Rocky explained that he could not live without her and that he had made mistakes and that he respected her, that he was scared about the future for them, for him, and for her. Her parents tried to send him on his way lying to him. They explained that Lucy was gathering her things back at the house. At first glance, he appeared to buy this.

As Rocky turned to head back to the house, with a slight gleam of hope in his eye, her parents added one last bit of their own opinion. "If you truly respect her, you'll respect the restraining order and Lucy's wishes for some time away."

Rocky spun back slowly. He stared, almost through them.

Lucy heard screams - loud, bloodcurdling screams - then nothing.

She gave it sometime then slowly, quietly ascended the basement staircase. Horrible thoughts ran through her mind. What if Rocky flipped again and left them for dead? What if he had them at gunpoint?

They were gone; the door swung ajar. A crude heart was scratched onto the floor under drops of blood.

Lucy didn't panic. She didn't show much emotion at all as a matter of fact. She reached for the keys on the end table and made her way to the car. She knew exactly where he was going with her parents: Where the heart is…at home.

# WAR IS MURDER

**One Month Ago**

I had been counting down the days until I could make my first find.

I had been studying the Battle of Antietam for as long as I can remember. I can't even say why but I was always drawn to this area and this event in particular. Perhaps it was the tagline of "Bloodiest Day in American History." Sure, this is macabre and maybe a little sick but it grabbed my attention, as with a multitude of Americans, hell the world.

I'm far from any professional in history. It's rather an intense hobby but living about a half hour away in Martinsburg helped make this easier and more accessible. This may have been a trickle down from my father's interest in the Civil War in general, who's really to say.

My reputation as an amateur historian made its way around the area. The nearby town of Sharpsburg was not very big, I'd guess a population of maybe 500 people. This reputation more often than not was negative. Afterall, these people and their property stretched back generations, back to the Civil War and that brutal battle in fact. They thought they knew more than any history book or outsider could ever know. At first this irritated me, not necessarily made me mad, but rather disappointed. Eventually I just learned to live with it and took the advantages when I could when someone was interested in talking to me or showing me the lesser-known locations of the battle. These were minimal and never really amounted to much, that is until a property right on the battlefield sold.

This property was owned by the same family dating far before the war ravaged the area, so this was a refreshing change. I believe the family name was Roulette but aside from being a bunch of old farmers who used to supply the entire state with everything from fruits to grain to beef. But that was way back when, since the Civil War, their land has been dead and unusable. They've pretty much lived off the government's compensation for lives. At least, that's what the locals say.

Ironically, the property was sold to a former Gettysburg College professor who was just as curious - scratch that - even more curious about the land and battle of Antietam than I am. My contacts throughout the town finally came through in a positive way for me as the new owner, Mr. Bradley Thompson actually called me! Don't get me wrong, I would have dug into the public records and found out who he was eventually, but this surely fast tracked all that mundane and tedious work.

After driving over and meeting Mr. Thompson one evening and sharing some good wine he brought in from the Adams County Winery, we discussed the proverbial elephant in the room. Before I could awkwardly approach the topic of breaking ground or simply relic hunting, the new landowner asked simply and with a smirk: "When do you want to start?"

I completely froze. "Start what?" I asked a little timidly. I shifted in my well-made Adirondack chair. How could he have known?

He chuckled as he pulled out a pair of muddy brown, thick cigars from his chest pocket. He passed one to me as I graciously reached over to grab it. I didn't smoke but accepted the gift regardless. "C'mon lad" he spoke in a boisterous Irish accent, "Your name just kept coming up when I asked around, so I had to at least give you a shot." He bit off the end of the cigar and spit the guts into the unlit fire pit. "Spoiler alert, you passed."

I tried to mimic his action and simply shredded the end of the cigar. With my cheeks flushing I choked and asked, "What did you ask?"

"Son," a thick puff of dark smoke rolls out between his puckered lips, "Does it matter? I know what you want. You want your moment. You want to find something, uncover something, discover something." His smirk gave me goosebumps as I gave a visible shiver. "I know you. You're exactly like me."

Mr. Thompson was not wrong. All I ever wanted to do was leave my name in a history book. God knew I wasn't going to do it working in construction. I never really thought this type of moment would come so I didn't exactly have any words. I gulped, still struggling with the torn cigar skin in my teeth, well throat now. "Give me a week and I can start." *Start what?* I thought to myself, but I wasn't going to question it. I was in. He was right, I wanted to discover something. And boy did I.

## Current Day

My research and minor excavation were fruitless. I utilized everything from the library, the research center, professors, everything short of time travel. Mr. Thompson's property seemed to be neglected from the majority of history books even though it was a fact, well local and verbal fact passed down generations, that this property and farmhouse was in full operation during the battle of Antietam.

The day I was going to sit down with Bradley and discuss this lack of success, I feared that would be the end of this venture. However, as I was on my way into the farmhouse, I stopped by truck to grab a jacket. I unlocked and sat in the driver's seat, allowed myself to take a breath and gather my thoughts and I paused. What was I looking at? A small white handkerchief was blowing under my windshield wipers. Definitely not mine. I grabbed it without thinking and headed into the farmhouse in search of Bradley. Naturally, I forgot my jacket.

Bradley shouted in from the office or library, he referred to this room as both, "In my library my mucker." That's not the first time he used that word; I still had no idea what it meant. I slowly poked my head in and without even making a sound he exclaimed "Come in, come in, pour yourself a pint of the black stuff" as he motioned to his refrigerator stocked full of Guinness.

"Uhh, no thank you" I stuttered embarrassingly. "I just wanted to apolo - "His look stopped me from apologizing for my failure. He was staring at the white cloth.

He reached out his hand without a word and, without hesitation, I handed it to him ever so gingerly. "So, you *finally* found something!" he thickly enunciated the 'finally' with his Irish drawl. "Look at that…" Bradley held it up to the light while pinching it with a pair of pencils using them in lieu of tweezers. A large red square practically outlined the white cloth with a spotting of a thick red mark toward one corner. I squinted trying to get a better look but before I could say a word Bradley proclaimed his excitement with "The Copse of trees!" as he nearly jumped out of his seat. Unfortunately, he did spill his Guinness which clearly upset him.

## Late September 1862

Blood still pooled all around the farmland. The stench of rotting corpses stung their nostrils and never really improved. Even though it had been two weeks since the horrific incident that cut through the entire area leaving a wake of destruction, the town was in shambles. The Battle of

Antietam ripped a hole in the heart of the young United States. This was the moment that would truly force the American people, regardless of which side of the conflict they supported, to see the carnage and death that the youth of this country was inflicting upon itself.

Eventually to be dubbed 'The bloodiest day in American history' a mere two weeks following the Battle of Antietam which cost 23,000 Americans their lives would also leave the area surrounding Sharpsburg, Maryland in complete disarray. This was no more evident than the mounds of bodies piled all throughout the woods and farmland. As the war raged on, this left the townspeople to contend with the unfortunate and disgusting endeavor of burying bodies they left behind.

The Roulette Farm, which truly supplied the entire area with their livestock, and really brought in massive trade from around the area was no exception. What was different here though is that the ground was scorched, the crops were destroyed, and their livestock was stolen by the retreating Union army. The young family was decimated. At the time of the Civil war, William and Margaret Roulette owned and operated the property. The pair had just had their third child in the months leading up to this conflict and were thriving. At least, that's what the community thought.

Following the birth of their third child, William began to sell off livestock and some of the new equipment his father-in-law had invested in before he unceremoniously passed the property to his daughter and her husband. This was only the start of the dismantling of the property in William's mind. He was a businessman, not a farmer. Sure, this was a fruitful farm but the time of slave-run farms was clearly coming to an end despite William's persistent disagreements. But none of that mattered now, the entire property including anything and everything that was worth even a cent was destroyed. He had nothing left.

Luckily for the Roulette's, Margaret's father John Miller, had made quite a name for himself not just with the farmland and supplying the town with cheap (near free prices in William's mind) produce but also acting as a preacher for the nearby Dunker Church and even councilman for the township. His representation helped lead the area in an anti-slavery movement. He was Confederate at heart but still believed in human rights.

William disagreed with pretty much everything his father-in-law stood for and, in his mind, would be his undoing and would guide his town toward a new cause and perhaps even a seceding of their own. Even though he had just recently begun to put his plans into action, the Civil War truly put an end to all of this. And now, he was forced to carry swollen, rotting corpses into a shallow grave. How did his life come to this?

Margaret watched from afar with an underlying smile, one she would never allow William to see. She knew his plans but thank God for this conflict, this bloody, brutal death riddled conflict. It not only drew her beloved's focus to saving every remnant of their property but it would help him see the beauty and benefit of this community. Their land was strewn with the dead, but on top of that the entire community came to help clean up the wreckage knowing what the Roulette land meant to them and how much her father did for them in the past. Even if this was the last gesture they ever received, it would be worth it.

A partially sunken piece of land was now visible now that the gun fire, smoke, and cannonade had cleared the formerly overgrown area of debris. Margaret gently pushed her husband into minimally excavating this spot

and developing a mass grave here for casualties of both sides of the country.
This would allow him to do even less work and cover up an area which was completely useless as it was prior to the war.

The entire community took it upon themselves to haul the mass amounts of dead to this spot once William had finished digging down maybe three feet. He was confident this was deep enough as he began to hit a thick layer of soil or roots, he wasn't sure but he knew that was more than enough to get rid of the stench and horrific sights - for now.

**Current Day**

Bradley and I trudged back to the sole grouping on trees on the property. He showed me the cloth and the red marks utilizing them as a type of guidance. "This is it." He dropped his hand and bowed as if he was a butler allowing me entrance.

"Mr. Thompson," I paused before I continued to see how he would react to this delay but he didn't react in the least, he simply stared at the unkempt, overgrown Copse of trees. "How does a garage rag tell you that this is…well…anything?" I looked down at my feet scared of his reaction.

Bradley Thompson, the eccentric Irish professor moved at a very young age from the Motherland to the infamous town of Gettysburg, Pennsylvania and practically grew up studying the Civil War. The first time he picked up a book referencing his displaced hometown he was drawn in. His interest piqued with the unknowns of the era with everything passed down, typically documented by the victors or each battle. He felt a pull into this like it was one of the great mysteries of the

American age. He felt like an explorer in the western frontier, or like his forefathers back in the old Ireland.

At my questioning, he was unwavering, "Unload your gear here, son." He didn't flinch at the question, nor did he really take much notice. It's as if that old, worn rag was what he was waiting for.

With my need to please and to stay employed in this venture, I did as asked. With my metal detector, LIDAR scanner, and satellite imagery I struck gold (sorry for the bad pun) right off the bat. By doing a simple sweep with my high end Minelab Equinox 800 Multi-IQ I began getting a slew of detections. This occurred before Bradley left which ultimately prompted him to stay for the duration of my scans. With these hits on the metal detector, I utilized my LIDAR scanner to pinpoint locations where there were disturbances in the ground beneath us. This spot seemed to be home to an entire cavern.

Bradley's eyes could have popped out of his head with how far they opened. Without delay he simply asked "What are you waiting for mucker? Give me a shovel! Dig!"

**Early October 1862**

The hole was opened and bodies casually thrown in. William paused, placed his hat and hand over his chest, asked the remaining townsfolk to join him, and said a short but meaningful prayer prior to covering them over. Before any of them had a chance to pick up their shovels to finish the job, Margaret stormed out of the farmhouse.

"William!" she scowled, making every man in the group cower in an awe-inspiring silence. "I told you to stop before putting those bodies in that hole!" She trampled toward the group, through the combination of mud and blood.

William puffed his chest and prepared to put up an unnecessary fight but backed down without the energy or care to do so. He simply dropped his shovel. Her look practically forced the group to do the same. "Fine. We'll finish tomorrow." He didn't say another word nor did he question her strange request. His walk back to the house reminded some of the onlookers of an old mule preparing itself to be put to rest after its lifetime of servitude. The contingent broke off and dispersed to their own homes after Margaret thanked them for their hours and hours of help and her gratitude by inviting them over for dinner and coffee some evening. This is typically the man's place but she took it upon herself to act accordingly ever since her father's passing years ago.

That evening, the sky opened up and the lightning raged as if God was mourning this massive death toll. The children were put to bed and William took up his typical evening perch in front of the fireplace, reading his papers on the town and surrounding boroughs. Even though it did not occur this night, not yet, his stereotypical nightcap would force him asleep in his sheepskin lounge chair. Margaret counted on this as she would use this time to get a much-needed break from the children's chaos, her husband's inadequacies, and just life in general. This is the timeframe she managed to solidify her future plans and how to continue the farm running. It was her responsibility apparently. To keep their family fed and recover from the damages sustained from this pointless, idiotic war. She would disappear to no one's surprise during this time so when she was unaccounted for that evening, no one was the wiser.

Margaret topped William's scotch off and backed away into the darkness. She gave him a few moments to down his sauce then she suited up in his boots, overcoat, and ranch hat.

As she slipped out the back door, her only visibility was that of her memory. Margaret miraculously found her way to the mound of death and decay and stepped around this hillside. She reached for her husband's shovel and slammed it into the muddied ground beneath her splashing the dark brown slush onto her white dress which, she had already thought about and planned out, she would burn if any of this mess grew too explainable.

**Current Day**

I found all of this out prior to our dig but Bradley Thompson's Civil War obsession did not stop there. Rather it stemmed into the Irish Brigade, deep into their ranks. In fact, he dug so deep that he uncovered a tie to the brigade. His ancestors, two great uncles, both served in the war and in that ruthless, courageous corp. They were on the forefront of many of the major battles of the Civil War, turning the tide for the Union and helping to solidify the United States of America. His relatives were both notated in battles leading up to Antietam but following this, they were never spoken about or documented again.

Charles and Frank O'Connor were both enlisted through the New York 69th, practically recruited right off the boat. Their names were synonymous, amongst their peers, with courage and valor. Unfortunately, they were practically erased from any documents including letters and journals on this fateful day. The pair was recorded "officially" as missing in action and presumed dead.

The majority of the Irish Brigade would carry letters with them into battle in case they were killed paired up with bibles, crucifixes, and rosaries. More often than not, these artifacts would be recovered by both sides out of respect upon burial. With the O'Conner brothers, however, their personal effects were never gathered nor were their letters sent home.

This was a true, albeit forgotten, mystery until Bradley Thompson began his research. As he backtracked through journals regarding his forsaken uncles, he was able to trace their comrades and even made contact with some of their families. With verbal stories, nothing documented or confirmed, Bradley was eventually pointed toward the Sharpsburg area and a newspaper clipping of the time ripped carelessly from a local paper. This clip was wrapped in a torn white cloth with a red handprint etched into it. The clipping read 'Maryland Missing!' and 'Suspect on the Loose!'

As Bradley pulled and saved these, he continued this search, ultimately bringing him full circle back to Gettysburg. In a nearby bed and breakfast, he was granted access to their historical documentation and dug out further white cloth reminiscent of the other shrouds he found. In each of these, more newspaper clippings provided more headlines of 'Multiple Found Dead!' and 'Killer on the Loose in Maryland?'

Eventually these contacts each guided him to the Battle of Antietam where every single headline stopped. There was never another one past the month of September of 1862. Could this be just unfortunate irony or was there something more to all of this? The only way he could continue his research was to be there, actually live in Sharpsburg. With one of the very few properties on the battlefield going up for sheriff sale, he immediately bought it and began recruiting help, whether they knew it or not; including me.

Our digging only got us so far. We had to hire an excavator but this also led to some red flags down the road. We took advantage of our time and this being private property but ultimately the excavator opened up the earth under that grouping of trees to uncover a mass gravesite. Each body had Irish Brigade type belongings. The metal detector was going haywire due to the slew of metal crosses and beads from long degraded rosaries. This made sense. What did not make sense was the bodies beneath them.

Once our initial dig was complete, the bodies with some type of recognition were all identified and tagged in some way. Most had the letters home whereas others had their names stitched into their berets.

This was only about 3-4 feet underground.

We could not break any ground beneath this, there was too much overgrowth which was odd. The excavator was brought back in to continue to break this barrier. As the operator finally broke through this layer of rock and roots and poorly laid concrete, we were finally getting somewhere. We both knew it.

"Halt!" an echoed voice blasted through a microphone. "This is the park rangers and we have with us the local PD." A siren sounded in their direction as if to prove this to us. "Stop what you are doing."

The excavator's arm lowered, bodies fell from it, rolling in the dirt and peering up at us from black, empty eye sockets.

**Late October, 1862**

As the month rolled on and the weather began to change, the community noticed a change in the Roulette household in both William and Margaret.

Following moving the hordes of bodies to the dig site, Margaret seemed to distance herself from the majority of the town. She pushed William to do most of the community outreach, which in her opinion was the way it was supposed to work anyway. And being so intertwined with the political side of the town, William removed himself from the farm and ceased selling off pieces and parts of the farmstead and rather hired out duties to keep the farm up and running. William's personality seemed altered, and he was very simplistic with no conversation, no opinions, just as if he were going through the motions. It was a perfect relationship - according to Margaret.

Her plan had worked out to a tee. That fateful night, following those bodies being moved to her requested location under the tree, she had the entire property to herself. She took advantage of this. She dug in further, with every shovel revealing not just roots or rocks or dirt but rather bones, shards, or broken and shattered pieces of bone. This did not startle her, rather it uncomfortably pleased her.

She continued to dig, tearing into the skeletal debris. Finally with dirt piled up around the outside, Margaret's shovel was thrown on top of that, followed by her dirt encrusted hand. As she stood above the makeshift grave, the moonlight spilled across her milky white skin and gleamed a dim blue light over the pit. Inside the dirt tomb, green tinted skin pocked with yellow dimples laid strewn about the pit. Arms crossed with legs, heads mixed in with torsos, a grotesque foot and hand combination all poured out in one fell swoop while Margaret stared down, a grin ear to ear, a gleam in her eye.

**Current Day**

After the smoke cleared and we were able to explain the situation, the park ranger and police force granted us access to examine the bodies. The agreement had to be made prior to us parting ways peacefully that we would return everything to the unmarked grave including the cadavers. Even though this tore us apart, Bradley and I agreed, whatever it took to examine some of these bodies.

We took advantage of the time provided and documented and photographed everything but the most startling discovery we made was not what they wore or who they were but rather *how* they died.

These bodies were still clad in tattered clothing but what was strange was that they were not wearing military garb. The soldiers buried above these poor souls were still wearing the gray and blue of typical Civil War uniforms. This tangle of twelve bodies was just downright gruesome. The body parts were dismembered and buried all throughout the hole completely devoid of respect or proper burial.

Upon close inspection of these bodies and the remaining clothing, the torsos were ripped open with what would have appeared to be the markings of a rib spreader, at least according to Bradley. How he knew that was beyond me.

The heads, well what remained of them, showed a brutality only seen in cinema. Nails, the old fashion wrought head type, were punctured all throughout each. Bradley assumed this was some type of torturous means the way these were applied followed only by their decapitations.

Oddly enough, the hands and feet seemed to be missing portions of each extremity. They were rather well preserved and showed extreme amputations of not just fingers or toes, but rather entire portions of hands and feet were removed. This again was surmised by Bradley to be torture techniques.

All in all, it was unknown whether the metal detector picked up the Irish Brigade's artifacts or these brutal metallic torture remnants. Regardless, when we were all done with our exhumations and inspections, we prepared to re-inter them.

As I turned back to get out of the way of the excavator, my last memory at that moment was a purple and red hued view of Bradley standing atop the dirt mound with the newly risen moon's light with a grin ear to ear, a gleam in his eye.

**Early November 1862**

A drunken and bow-legged William approached Margaret from behind. He glanced over her shoulder and spewed his last scotch all across her boots. She glanced over her shoulder as if she expected him. "Help me my darling" she practically cackled.

His eyes grew wide, and his voice trembled, "So it is true…it was you…"

"You know what I'm capable of," Margaret gloated, "how could you ever doubt my prowess?" Lightning cracked and lit the sky behind her. "Now fill this hole and dump the bodies."

Without any argument (how could he have any at this point?) William grabbed a shovel and began filling the carcasses with anything he could loosen up, broken stone, cement slabs, trees, bushes, roots.

After hours of this task, and Margaret simply staring at him or into the darkness it was difficult if not impossible to tell, William finally had the lower level covered with rubble and another layer of those poor Irish lads dumped on top. He started to knock the dirt in to finalize this horrific act just as the rain started to pound hard around them.

"That's enough," Margaret softly and calmly explained. "Mother Nature will do the rest. Now come, we have plenty to discuss." She turned back to the farmhouse before William could respond. He followed her like a scalded dog.

At their meager kitchen table, Margaret laid out a handful of newspaper clippings. Each explained a different crime seemingly unrelated. There were disappearances, robberies, accidental deaths, suicides, and even some notating the potential for a murderer on the loose. "I saved each one," she calmly explained. "Before the war, leading up to our little piece of hell on Earth, this has been going on for nearly ten years."

William couldn't believe any of it. His face pale, stomach twisted; he was unsure if it was his horror and disgust or his alcohol reacting to a weak constitution. "You did all of these?" He peered at the papers dating back to 1854, all from the same Sharpsburg post.

"Now I'm done." She looked longingly out a window at the rolling storm clouds. "At least here." Her pause felt like an eternity. "I'm going home, back to Ireland. It will be safer there. These people are starting to suspect something, but this war came at a perfect time. I can use it to disappear and bury my tracks." Another pause, allowing for even more time for

William's stomach to churn. "Don't worry though," Margaret warned her hand in the air as if swatting a fly, "you can keep the land and the farm and do what you will with it. My father would roll over in his grave if he knew I was doing this but hell, he would have rolled ten times over knowing his own daughter stabbed him in the back bringing down his glass castle."

A sigh was released from his bowels but then panic struck him. "And what should I tell everyone? And what if they start asking questions?"

She wrinkled her nose and pursed her lips. "I don't rightfully care to be completely honest with you my dear. Tell them I was afraid of that hellish war. Tell them I'm going to check on my mother after I lost my brothers. Stupid boys fighting in war they don't have any part in," a tear actually seemed to build up in her eye, "dammit Charley, Franky…" Margaret immediately made her way to her bags which were already partially packed. "I'm taking the children though, you are aware of that, no?"

William pushed his chair back as if he was prepared to stand yet no feeling could be had in his legs and not an ounce of bravery was left in him. "Fine," he huffed, "just don't hurt them. Please, to God, whatever you do, just don't hurt them."

Margaret scoffed, "Hurt my own children? What do you take me for? A monster?" She shuffled out of the room to gather her children and a few final pieces of jewelry and keepsakes.

As he found himself alone, William grabbed a few of the newspaper clippings and rolled them up. He quickly tore a piece of his tattered shirt and folded a few into it. He tossed it under the rug in the middle of the floor. He then repeated this, throwing a few more pieces in another folded cloth then out the window. Theirs would eventually be buried with the remaining soldiers. As he ripped this piece, he cut his palm on his hunting knife. Even though he tried to stop the bleeding with this ragged cloth, it would ultimately take a lot more than simple pressure and even need some medication to heal. The final shroud was concealed in another ripped fabric and hidden within Margaret's packed bag, and he was lucky enough to have this travel all the way back to Ireland with her.

Not much more was ever said following that moment, but William managed to rebuild in time. Ironically, he made that farm one of the most profitable in the entire state and even kept it in the family for generations to come. Even though Margaret never returned, William remarried. His new wife would allow things to remain somewhat similar if not confusing and blurred the lines of fact and fiction as her name, too, was Margaret. The couple had two children of their own who would grow up on that farm, little known to them for the tragedy that befell their father and never knew of their step siblings or their father's first marriage.

## Current Day

As my vision came back to be, a little blurry but manageable, I could make out the dark silhouette of Bradley standing over me with a blood-soaked shovel in hand. "What…" is all I could make out with a gargled breath.

"Quiet" Mr. Thompson pressed a finger to his lips as he glanced around. "Wait," he chuckled.

I knew there were others around, the excavator at least close by and the cop and ranger hopefully in shouting distance. "Help" I groaned through clenched teeth.

"Lad," his smile was so putrid so disturbing it just tore into my soul. He disappeared for a moment over the dirt mound. Rather than reappearing, the body lunges down the hillside pulling dirt and debris with it. The lifeless body was still wearing a tattered orange vest and white construction hard hat which had been busted up (more like busted in). Blood poured out from his torn open gut, allowing his insides to follow suit. The excavator was no more. "There's no one around to help." His voice was calm and confident. "Save your breath my mucker," his voice echoed as another body rolled down the now blood-stained dirt wall.

As the body finally fell silent, I noticed the light green park ranger uniform and golden name badge glinting in the moon but the main grotesque feature; it was missing its head. I let out a distressed grunt, but the blood loss was starting to affect me and I could barely move. My limbs felt weak, the pain struck me in waves as the blood continued to trickle from the open gash on my forehead.

My last hope was the cop, maybe this Irish maniac would have had the intelligence to avoid any conflict with the law. These hopes were immediately dashed as a round object, covered in blood but appeared as a disturbing black hue in the darkness. It laid at my feet; it wasn't just dismembered either. It was crudely pierced with rust coated nails.

I powered back up into the darkness expecting Mr. Thompson to finish the job or bury me alive. At this point the pain and fear swirled and created an unbearable combination and the only thing I could think of keeping me alive was this inhumane, unnatural adrenaline rush. I would have preferred a quick death but at this given moment, any type would be a blessing. My eyes must have blurred again, I was seeing double.

"Officer O'Connor," Mr. Thompson placed his hand on the cop's shoulder and looked in his direction, "Cousin."

My heart dropped. "How? Why?" my list of questions could have continued on, but I stopped as my body forced me to, uncontrollably so.

The duo above me snickered, Officer O'Connor still had not said a word and I doubted I'd ever hear his voice but Mr. Thompson's booming, vicious voice overshadowed the thunderstorm fast approaching. "Laddy, you'll never be remembered for any discovery. No important find or historical documentation. No, no, rather you'll be forgotten just like these lost souls, and you'll be a mere footnote in my family's history. You see, my mother started this burial plot long before the great Civil War and that damn ruinous Battle of Antietam. I'm simply tying up her loose ends."

"Me?" I racked my brain. I couldn't figure it out, how was I, a nobody, a loose end? How was I tied into this sick and twisted tale?

Mr. Thompson took a few steps down into the pit then slid the rest of the way, just to stare me down nice and close. "My Great Grandmother, Margaret Miller, had an estranged husband. He remarried and had some children of his own. The strange part is that they disappeared without a trace. They were displaced, seemingly hidden." He took a breath then stepped back. His confidence could be not just seen but physically felt with an electricity of sorts in the air. "Hidden, until just a month ago. And now, I will bury those last remnants of her disgraced past."

Without breaking eye contact, Mr. Bradley Thompson raised his arm, motioning to his cousin and local law enforcement, Officer O'Conner. A purring engine echoed over the hillside and loud beeping surrounded the area. A metallic spout appeared at the crest of the dirt mound. Mr.

171

Thompson heaved his way back up the hill as a slushy, gray compound poured out of the cylinder.

My cement tomb poured around me, my last vision was that of lightning crashing behind Mr. Bradley Thompson, but my blurred vision must have begun to take over once again because I could have swore I saw a woman with muddy boots and bloodied white dress standing right next to him. The pair was cackling away under the blue hue of the full moon which rose high behind them while their grins glistened in the pale light just as the cement swallowed the remainder of my body and my entire existence blinked away in one final cry of pain, suffering, but worse yet a deep seeded fear of being forgotten.

# SHADOW IN THE WOODS

I knew I was going to die.

My blood pumped, my veins swelled and sweat poured through every pore in my body. I ducked below branches and jumped over fallen logs. The darkness grew closer. I could hear the unsettling growls, smell the putrid odor, and feel the ground shake with every step this creature took.

There was nowhere I could go, nothing I could do, so I ran. The towering beast tore a hole through the overgrowth as it grew closer. So, I ran.

The shadow of this beast stretched over seven feet tall, and, to me, that was a low estimate. Its black hair glistened in the moonlight as I glanced over my shoulder. The thing's muscular arms pulled aside thick tree trunks, snapping them like twigs. What sent shivers up my spine was the fact that it actually had two pairs of these massive limbs!

As it grew closer, the creature's jagged fangs pierced through its demented grin. The growls echoed and vibrated my soul, sending an invisible blast through my head. Its shrieks, if you could consider them that, produced pure terror and silenced the entirety of the woodlands, scaring off any wildlife with a half of a brain.

At the singular moment, I thought I was truly done for, an opening emerged in the heavily wooded area. I burst through the final shards of wooded fingers and nearly catapulted myself into a towering flame. I glanced around, slowly at first, in hopes of finding someone. My hollow cries echoed to no avail. I stood across the flames as if it was a shield. Until my eyesight focused beyond the flame.

A mutilated torso hung from the crooked branches. Pools of blood surrounded it. The carcass was completely unrecognizable. One arm dangled down toward the ground while both feet were grotesquely amputated. I spewed my dinner right into the fire forcing the flames to turn a bluish hue and vault toward the open canopy above the opening.

The sudden burst forced me to my knees. The growl echoed through the woods, piercing my auditory perception. As I covered my ears, tears poured from my eyes and blurred my vision. While staring back toward the macabre scene I noticed an outstanding marking on the corpse's chest. A phrase of 'Heart Means Everything' is tattooed over what was once a beating heart. It was underlined by three thick, crude lines. I reached down toward my own chest revealing my matching identical tattoo. My brother!

I spun around but as I twirled in hopes of running further from this horrific display my eyes glued to an even worse depiction of mutilation and inhumane torture. Three more bodies lay in the edge of the clearing. All of their heads were removed leaving blood spewing from dark red stumps. Stick pikes lined the clearing just beyond these, each with a head coarsely bored through each showing the tops of the makeshift spears jutting all the way through the tops.

My brother's head was forced toward the bottom of the shaft causing his eyes to protrude out in such a grotesque manner.

The trees were forced aside behind me. I fell back towards my best friend, or at least what was left of him. The orange eyes were the first detail I could make out. Blood dripped from its fangs while dirt and grime were ingrained in its thick black fur. Its muscular frame loomed over me as I noticed the creature's legs were bent in the opposite direction, almost that of a canine.

I crawled backward toward the woods once more while tears, blood, and sweat all nearly blinded me. I knew I was going to die. There was no way to survive this.

I made it to my feet as the beast's jaw dropped open. It must have been some type of double hinge feature to allow it to take larger bites of its victims or even swallow smaller prey in one gulp. The growl this time deafened me, as all I could hear was a shrill ringing in my head. The adrenaline must have taken hold of me as I rushed off into the blackness.

Whatever happened next was, and still is, a mystery to me. I ran perhaps for five more minutes. I know the brush whipped my face and cut my cheeks. Vines and thorns coarsely ripped at my clothing and forced open new wounds. The last thing I remembered was just a bright light engulfing me…

- One Year Following My Brother's Death-

"You do know that sounds absolutely insane, right?" The man's gruff voice sent chills down my spine. He just shrugged me off. "I've been researching cryptids and undocumented animals of this region for nearly thirty years." He tapped his pen on my map. "You're telling me that just outside this campground there was a massacre…"

I snatched the pen from him, and I scribbled a circle just outside the Laurel Ridge State Park. Even though I knew this wasn't an exact location, I know where we set up camp and I vividly remembered the signs for the nearby town of Ligonier.

"It was right here." I must have sounded partially insane, partially irritated. It was a mere six-month gap from the time of my brother's demise until I met this confident, albeit cocky, cryptozoologist. I pushed the map back towards him, knocking his nameplate onto the floor. I paused, took a breath, and reached down to pick it back up. I brushed it off and had it gleaming in the fluorescent lights, highlighting his title plate of 'Dr. Thomas R. Schantz.'

He ran his fingers through his whitened goatee and affixed his fancy name plate back on his table. "Listen, kid," he looked off into the distance. I didn't take offense even though I was far from a 'kid.' I was just hoping for the best from this renowned professional in this field of the paranormal. His recent book on the Ohio Frogman just rocketed to the top of the charts as he was just coming off a hit documentary focused on the Jersey Devil. I held my breath awaiting his response. "I'm sorry for your loss. I know you've really been through it here. Your brother, that ghastly scene you recall, but I've been there. I know this area. My family first settled in the nearby town of Johnstown. He pointed to the town just east of that hellacious memory. "Even though they changed the name from Schantztown to Johnstown but…" his cheeks flushed "I digress."

I put my hands up as if preparing to surrender. "I just need help. You're the only expert from the area. I want to know what that was and just where all of the evidence went."

Dr. Schantz interlocked his fingers and sat back. "That's just it. There's no trace of anything. The story you told me, the same exact one you told the police, there's just nothing that fits the description. And as far as whatever that cryptid might be, well…" once more he trailed off and puffed his cheeks outward as if at a loss for words.

"I will pay for your time. Whatever that might be." I was ready to beg. For my sake, for my parents' sake, for my brothers' family's sake. "I'll pay for lodging, food, everything. I want to show you the spot. I want your opinions. I want you to take this seriously, more so than the damn cops. That's all I ask." I stepped back and waited for him to just say 'No' and send me on my way.

The 'Cryptid Hunter,' as he was known, leaned forward and slid me his business card. He flipped it over and scribbled another number on it. "This is my personal number. Give me six months until I finish this ParaCon tour and call me. We'll meet up and see if we can figure something out." He grabbed a book off the stack next to him, cracked it open, and signed it. "For your perseverance, kid."

---

I barely made it that half a year until I called him. His phone barely rang twice as he answered.

"It's you, isn't it?" His gruff voice almost choked through the phone. He puffed his cigarette into the receiver, "I can't go with you." There was a long pause. "But I'll teach you everything I know."

---

He was dying. I could tell by the look in his eyes. He was getting weaker with every passing hour. Cancer. Go figure. The poor soul gets his fame, his notoriety, people finally take him seriously, then this. The reason he couldn't go was not because he did not believe me or wanted to go but he physically could not go.

We sat in his office just overlooking the downtown area of Pittsburgh. Carnegie Mellon University had just recently opened its doors to his specialty. He was offered a full-time position as a professor in cryptid sciences and the documentation and study of unknown species. This would become my mainstay for research for the next year.

Even though we had plenty to cover, and we would, we ended every week with the beast I encountered which took my brother away from me. The normal routine was to go over my story, detail by detail for hours. What I learned was much more than I ever anticipated, and I ultimately wrote a thesis on this monstrosity while earning my Master's degree from Carnegie Mellon University.

Thomas Schantz was only given about six months to live. What the doctors didn't realize is that his mental state was so much stronger than anticipated. Pair that miracle with fate and he pulled through for three more years! He followed through with his promise of teaching me everything he knew, from the infamous Skinwalker to the lesser-known cryptids of the New York Lizardman.

The most compelling of our research and my absorption of knowledge was an unnamed cryptid. We nicknamed it the American Rubezahl. The Rubezahl was of German ancestry, but little was known of it. Thomas was obsessed with this shapeshifting beast which his mother had told him stories of as a child. It's unknown what exactly a Rubezahl was but legend says it's a large beast with a tail, animal legs, and sometimes depicted with antlers. Typically, the Rubezahl was considered a giant which would chase miners out of their woodland areas and sometimes even out of towns leaving them permanently abandoned. Even though we never truly made any further evidence-based claims, our research guided us to its background and story as best we could. The name of 'Ruby' eventually stuck for our research group spawning a Nessie-esque nickname for the creature.

Eventually, upon Thomas' passing, I set out on a true continuous investigation of the area in no small part due to his inheritance being redirected toward my sole possession. This allowed me to purchase a local cabin and to afford to purchase my own equipment for endless hours of research.

Understandably this also created natural enemies for me and a true hindrance to the work at hand. A lawsuit and court battles with his son, Glenn, helped forge a hatred between the two of us which had no end in sight. Regardless, I pursued Thomas' true dream of uncovering a new cryptid and my pursuit of my brother's murderer.

Prior to striking out into the deep, dark woodlands, however, I would publish our findings along with Thomas' biography. Again, this added fuel to the fire as Glenn did not approve of this, nor did he agree with some of our research.

What began as a pet project and a way for Thomas to pass along his knowledge before he succumbed to the invisible death ended with an intense, and sometimes erratic, deep dive into the American Rubezahl including a visual description and a theoretical backstory.

- American Rubezahl; Published Five Years Following My Brothers' Death -

The end of World War II saw the rise of Operation Overcast. This top secret and classified government program helped lawfully, albeit secretly, import the top German Nazi scientists and physicists into America. While the majority of these scientists studied and documented weaponry and medicine, those imported into the northwestern United States found a home in a string of underground bunkers. A portion of these bunkers have been declassified and actually open to the public. These locations were nicknamed the Alvira Bunkers.

What is not known to the public, and has been completely blocked off, even to the extent of being demolished, is the second layer of bunkers. This next level was host to laboratories and heavy duty. We could not verify this on our own but with the help of notorious urban explorers, we were able to document these through videos and photographs. Unfortunately, those who explored these areas perished due to nuclear radiation and they passed away under the most extreme pain and discomfort.

This gave way to the theories of genome splicing and DNA recreation. What is utilized today, legally, is not nearly strong enough to build new DNA. What we found with this research is that nuclear power helped push the limits and actually allowed for DNA splicing.

Paperwork and documentation extracted from these bunkers showed successful mutation of animal and human hybrids. This seemed to pique toward the end of the Cold War leading to these hybrid creature programs losing all control of both the beasts which were created as well as the funding which dried up quite abruptly. This is partially why these bunkers were just closed off and the entrances destroyed rather than dismantled or shipped off to other government facilities.

With a handful of the documentation and after interviewing a few active scientists we were able to piece some of things together. Based on the handwritten notes, we managed to piece together the ultimate goal at Alvira, to hybridize a wolf, a bear, and a human. While the majority of these attempts were fruitless, causing nothing but needless pain and exorbitant amounts of fear in their subjects, there eventually was progress.

The countless bodies left in the wake of this progress were adding up and the facility ran behind on burning these failures in their kiln so as these failed experiments piled up, the bodies were stacked in a freezer. As an added precaution, the creature's heads were removed and piled up right next to these bodies. This horrific scene of blood and gore may have added to the successful creation's insane mindset.

While the monster had already jolted to life, still strapped to a table behind bulletproof glass doors, it had a perfect sightline to its fallen family. It's unknown and undocumented as to why they lost control, but the creature's strength easily overpowered any type of restraint or tranquilizers. It appeared as though the monster took a moment to focus and align its eyesight, but it's hypothesized that the beast's very first gaze was set on those failed creations with limbs strewn about and painful looks were pasted on their faces.

In no more than two minutes it's said that this unholy entity ripped from its straps, pounded an opening in the bulletproof glass, and feasted on any scientists that came in arm's length. The monster, with a bear's strength, wolf's agility, and human's mind, cut down anyone that may have deemed an enemy whether they had pointed a gun at it or held their hands up in surrender. There was no mercy. This beastly monstrosity left a mass of despair; heads decapitated, limbs torn from torsos, intestines yanked from cavities.

There were minimal survivors but those who survived seemed to believe that this creature let them live. The three that were left alive were each disfigured in some way, each in a different manner, but all of them described the exact same sensation. The monster stared at them with its orange piercing eyes, as if looking into their souls. This moment was said to make their bodies burn. As they left eye contact, they were released from this pain and seemingly knocked unconscious, completely drained of energy.

There was no documentation as to what followed. It's unknown if they tracked this beast down. If it escaped. Where it went. Nothing. Nothing, except one newspaper article which described a rash of murders each leaving bodies dismembered, campsites ravaged, and just an overall sense of chaos unleashed in the area. These locations covered multiple areas throughout this state park area but there is no other documentation found of this incident and a retraction article calling the previous writing an 'Unfortunate mishap by a disgruntled employee.'

### - Ten Years Following My Brother's Death-

Our research finally reached a point where I could not proceed any further without some type of hard evidence. The next logical step was to recreate the campsite from that fateful night. On the tenth anniversary of his death, I opted to return to that same exact camping spot where my brother took his last breath.

I managed to purchase brand new equipment to document any findings and everything mundane for a day-to-day authentication approach. While

I planned to stay out here myself, I did have some help making camp with some scientists who had owed Thomas over the years.

We kept the mood as light as possible with such a serious scenario laid out in front of us. From one of their pink jumpsuits to the stench of one of the assistant's dreadlocks poking from under his Rasta Cap we kept the jokes coming almost as a way to defuse the mounting tension. One other assistant showed up, but his newly found sales rep attitude wore thin on our group but did pay off as he packed his top-of-the-line cameras and motion activated sensors in his loosely knit bag, which naturally we managed to pull into the banter.

To add to my intrigue and timeframe here, there was a spike in missing hikers. In particular, these were recorded within a radius situated toward the outskirts of the protected wildlife area. With these I did opt to bring a firearm although I really hadn't planned on using it. My approach was always intended to be to document and evade with the majority of my supplies completely expendable.

As the sunset drew ever closer, an imminent sensation of dread dawned upon the group. I did not want these good Samaritans to be put in the way of any potential issues, so I sent them on their way as soon as camp was set and I was comfortable in my surroundings. I tossed a few bundles of cash inside each of their bags for their help. Once again, putting these remaining research funds once belonging to Thomas to use.

Sun began to set and the woodland fell under a thick sheet of darkness. Oddly enough, the silence was deafening. I could not hear any scurrying of critters, distant growls, or even the simple chirping of crickets. This was all odd and gave me vivid flashbacks to ten years prior but nothing would stop me from finding out more. Finding something on this creature and documenting anything I came across throughout my stay.

While the night dragged on and I fought to keep my eyes affixed on the cameras, I downed energy drinks to fight the natural urge to pass out. Not one creature appeared on any camera nor through any motion activated device. I wrote my memoirs to focus my attention here until a shriek cut through the stifling heat and stone-cold silence.

The shriek sent chills shudder down my spine but more than just the unsettling feeling of that inhuman growl it gave me flashbacks to the worst day of my life. If Deja Vu was real, this was a prime example of this unnatural occurrence. I kept a sharp eye on my tools but nothing was ever alerted but I was suddenly on edge.

I pulled the gun from its case and loaded the magazine with eight bullets and tossed a handful in my pocket. I was still uncertain about using it, that was not my intent by any means, but I also was not planning on being left as a helpless victim to any God-damned monster.

Another growl shook my tent, this time setting off every device at my disposal. My hand physically shook. I could feel that fear gripping me once again, all too similar to the incident ten years ago. I grabbed the pistol and stuffed it behind my back and covered it over with my flannel.

While I wanted to head toward the open tent flap my eyes were affixed to one camera which was focused just outside the open area of the campground. The trees could be seen shaking. I could feel heavy stomps and footfalls coming toward the area. I had no choice. There was one option. I had to face this. I had to do this for me, for Thomas, for my brother.

With a final chug of my Celsius energy drink, I pulled the pistol back out and aimed toward the door. I stepped out into the open air and immediately smelled the death waiting for me. It was unsettling and disturbing on a fundamental level. I peered around and headed for the opening where the trees flexed. One arm shoved aside the overgrowth while I led into the woods with the muzzle of the pistol.

There was no beast in my sight but there was a pool of blood leading into the darkness. What was more was four bloodied streaks as if someone was dragged out into the abyss. This was the only option, I had to follow this macabre sight as I prepared myself for anything that may come before me. What I did not expect was a single beam of light piercing through the darkness. It was strong enough to force me to wince and shield my eyes.

While I stepped toward this, still cocked and loaded, my stomach did not accept the macabre scene that was laid before me. The light was of a single flame shimmering atop of metallic spike. Blood soaked the dirt directly below me but created a deep pond around the pike. Just beyond this javelin buried in the ground were stacks of limbs crudely piled. Arms and legs, hands and feet, thighs and forearms, any grisly combination of these sickening dismemberments were mocking me.

I stepped backward but slipped on something soaked in blood. I glanced down and noticed a familiar knit bag. My eyesight reset at the glow of the open flame as I spotted a pink hoodie still draped on a torso, armless and headless, stained with a dark red, almost brown, wet coating. A crop of dreadlocks were wrapped inside a thorny bush just next to this sight, still encased in a now red Rasta Cap. Thomas' assistants were brutally murdered and carelessly thrown under the shadow of this flame.

Ruby was nearby, I knew it, but what kind of creature sets up these elaborate scenes? My head was spinning and blood was rushing to my head. I knew I was on the verge of passing out but I had to fight it or I would be lost to the depths of darkness. These people, these good-hearted people, would be lost. No one would ever know their story. Their families would never know what truly happened to them. I had to fight this. I had to get this tale known. Better yet, I had to take this creature's head back with me. I had to end this reign of terror.

I aimed the pistol upward toward the star-speckled sky. Without another moment's hesitation I pulled the trigger to call out this disturbing, cold-blooded creature. As I looked close at my comrades, I moved closer to ensure I filmed them with my mobile clip-on camera. The dismemberments felt off. I moved even closer and took to a knee to get an up-close inspection of the wounds.

The cuts caught my eye. They were too clean. They weren't torn apart. They were cleanly cut, almost surgically so. My head spun again; what was this thing?

As I stood, something shined just off in the darkness. It must have been the beasts' eyes. I recall its orange hue casting a spell on me and I did not want to get caught in these deadlights. Instead of waiting for the monster to pounce, I fired three shots at this evil glare.

Rather than sickening thuds of bullets piercing flesh as I was expecting there was a pinging of metal. I did a double take at this and moved toward it, once again caught completely off guard. As I pushed aside some of the underbrush, the light of the flame bounced off a silver gleam of a machete. My eyes were pulled just next to this at another shining metal. This one was attached to a crude wooden shaft; an ax.

Now my mind was reeling. A monster that used tools? Why would it need this? What was this - my thought was cut short by darkness and a loud ringing in my ears.

---

My eyesight was blurry and my ears were still echoing. I could taste blood on my lip. I tried to shake this off but it only made this sensation worse, almost giving me a vertigo feeling. I tried to reach for my pistol but my arms were restrained behind my back.

Now the monster used rope?!

Two echoing gunshots rang out immediately drawing my attention to the newly lit line of torches. Just behind these jumping lights I saw a shadow move. As it drew toward the light, two beady eyes pierced the darkness.

This was no beast. This was no creature. It was, however, certainly a monster.

Out of the darkness, Glenn sauntered slowly forward! Thomas' only son!

"Why?!" is all I could muster as I spit blood from my busted jaw.

His face, distorted and obviously crazed, moved closer toward me. I felt a heavy anger boil inside me. As his mouth opened to break the silence, he lurched forward and jumped to the tree I was bound to - no he didn't jump. Glenn was thrown!

There were no words, no explanation, barely a shriek. His head cracked against the tree just above my head. My immediate thought was: 'Good, serves you right!'

Just peeking out of the darkness, with a scruffy and white hood draped over his head, another large and towering mountain of a man stood. His long and thick beard jutted from this hooded figure's face, nearly coming to a point at his chest. Without a word he cuffed up his tattered sleeves revealing thick forearms; one draped in a wolf tattoo, the opposite with a growling bear.

He reached down at the lifeless body of Glenn and heaved him up without breaking a sweat. "I am redemption" his voice hissed. This behemoth slammed Glenn against the tree and with an open palm shoved his head into the thick of the tree. Rather than immediate or any blunt trauma, he seemingly gently cradled his head against the tree.

This goliath glared down toward me and pushed. Glenn's muffled groans were stifled as his skull creaked and cracked. I couldn't see this, but worse, I could feel this in my bones. The sound of popping and snapping echoed out of the hollow of the tree as the giant forced it even harder. Blood trickled from Glenn's ears dripping slowly down his cheeks. His nose began to spew blood as there was more cracking. His eyes bulged, blood compounding behind his orbital until finally the first one popped, exploding blood from one socket and covering me in a putrid slimy goo. Glenn tried to cry out but there was nothing left. His cranium popped once more forcing his cheekbones through the skin creating sharp knife-like apertures breaking through his skin and even piercing the tree. Blood poured, covering me a second skin, one sticky and slimy.

I turned my head to lose my stomach, just bile at this point, but as I did so, Glenn's body was dropped on top of me. I was buried in blood and gore.

"Do you know who I am?" this humongous man whispered. The sound of his voice was horrific in its own rite but as I glanced up at him seeing his beard jut out of the dirty brown-red hood forced me to slip into a semblance of insanity. "I am of the Schantz lineage. I am the heir, the bloodline." This beastly figure yanked his hood back to reveal long, scraggly hair. "And now, I am the only one."

My jaw, albeit knocked out of place, still found a way to drop. I sat in confusion. I could feel my face distort. All during this, I had the wherewithal to start jostling my wrists through the loosened rope. I knew he was about to get something off his chest. Therapy through violence I suppose.

This colossus of a man hissed through jagged teeth, "Thomas was my father." He crooked and elongated finger pointed down at Glenn's battered body and smashed head. "He didn't know we were step brothers. But then again," he took a deep breath, "you were more of a son than this chump I've heard."

"What? How?" I mumbled, barely audible.

He either heard my pathetic whisper or was planning on telling me regardless. "Thomas hid my mother. She was his mistress. Once he found out he impregnated her, he knew his reputation and personal life would be destroyed. Naturally, like any insecure, conceited, self-righteous piece of trash would do…" this beast finally showed some humanity as he shifted in his stoic stance and gulped hard. "He hid me. He paid my mother off and wrote regular checks to keep us surviving and quiet. Just barely, might I add." He reached down and grasped Glenn's collar with a singular hand. With minimal effort, he shuffled Glenn's lifeless ragdoll of a body across the opening toward the macabre scene of disgusting body parts. "We lived in this medieval, third world, second rate half-assed log cabin in the foothills of these here woods. But we managed. Her and I. Mother and son. A regular load of cash incoming monthly for food and necessities."

He spun back toward me, eyes locking on mine, piercing my soul. There was almost a sense of heated pain and hatred that glared into me, through the ether as if sucking my remaining lifeforce from me. I could say nothing. I couldn't move. I still squirmed and tried to wrench my hands free but to no avail. I felt the blood trickle down from my wrists but I was stuck. I had the sudden thought to reach for the pistol in hopes of finding a miracle. I must have shifted too much, though, making Thomas' long-lost son uneasy.

"No, no, no" he shook his head, his beard shooting from side to side. "You're not going anywhere!" He reached behind him pulling my pistol out. "And this?" The brute looked curiously at the gun as if never seeing one before. Suddenly, he tossed it toward the pile of amputated limbs. "You don't need that." He stepped toward me, finger pointing accusingly. "As I was saying before I was so rudely interrupted. You took it all away from me. Out of nowhere, the money stopped showing up. My father made one last visit to tell us the worst; that he was dying and that it came on fast. He'd be gone soon. He left us with one last bag of cash then disappeared…" He reached for a machete buried deep into a stump and raised it above his shoulder. "Only…" he slammed the machete down right above my neck, shredding a chunk of the tree into pieces spewing across my face. "He never died!" He yanked an ax from a stump next to me like it was butter. "And where was the money? Donated to research?!" He slammed it down into my thigh shooting a burning pain down my leg, up my thigh, and forcing tears down my cheeks and more blood spitting out of my busted mouth. "No! He gave it to you!"

All I could do was scream and writhe in pain. I couldn't move. I couldn't defend myself. I was helpless, nearly lifeless. The pain returned as he unceremoniously yanked the blade from my fresh wound. Blood burst from the gap, revealing muscle and bright red strands of fibrous tissue.

"And now," he raised his arm above his head, gripping the ax tight, "I get to be the last man standing." He released his arm, ready to drive the rusted shard of metal into my neck…

A black mass dove from the darkness sending this behemoth flailing. I thought the ax was going to kill me but now my gut really twisted and I knew exactly what I was looking at as it stood on its unnatural hind legs. This monster was so much worse than any inanimate object, no matter who was wielding it. My brother knew. This bastard man-child was about to find out.

Its orange gleaming eyes looked over its shoulder right at me. I thought I had an opening to escape but my God, those eyes…I froze.

The beast snapped its attention back to Thomas' nameless son as he attempted to pull himself up off the leaf bed. It did not give him an opportunity. It pounced. The black fur engulfed this man-beast as its claws swiped into his neck, sending blood into the air, a red mist surrounded the mass of gore. The creature drove its teeth into the man's jugular, nearly decapitating him with one blow. He couldn't even scream. He was coughing on his own blood.

During this disgusting massacre, I shimmied my way up the tree. I used the machete still lodged in the tree to cut myself loose. The gun still laid near the pile of bodies, my first instinct forced me to reach for the pistol. I knew I still had a few shots left. Seeing the two mutated beasts, I weighed my options. I stood no chance.

I ran. My leg gave out on me multiple times, this I knew, the pain was memorable to say the least. I only stopped long enough to tuck the gun back into my belt buckle.

---

I don't remember how I got here. I saw bright white lights and now I'm surrounded by doctors and nurses. The first IV bag is almost empty so I've started to come around. My gun is nowhere to be found, hell I was lucky to be aware enough to write this account on my makeshift tablet; the back of an intake form.

Hopefully I'll have some kind of answer soon - but - the growl. I can hear it; right? Is the monster coming for me? Or is that unsettling, disturbing, unnatural shriek stuck in my head.

I'll have an answer soon…

# About the Author

Derrick Smith is a horror author, seasoned paranormal investigator, and dedicated researcher based in Pittsburgh, Pennsylvania. As co-founder of Iron City Paranormal, he has spent over a decade documenting unexplained phenomena, blending hands-on field investigation with deep historical research to uncover the layers behind haunted locations. His dark fiction is rooted in reality, drawing inspiration from the true accounts, interviews, and evidence he gathers during his investigations.

Derrick's fascination with the paranormal began early. As a child, he had a life-altering encounter in the woods behind his family home: a vision of a Native American man kneeling beside a stream, silently dipping his hand into the water. The man appeared impossibly real, yet entirely out of place. That moment sparked a lifelong obsession with the unknown, planting the seed for a future of both storytelling and inquiry.

Beyond the supernatural, Derrick holds a bachelor's degree in project management and works professionally as a project manager for pathVu, a Pittsburgh-based startup committed to making cities more accessible through innovative pedestrian mapping. Whether managing large-scale tech projects or piecing together fragmented historical narratives, he approaches every challenge with curiosity, rigor, and a sharp analytical mind.

As a researcher, Derrick goes beyond ghost hunting. He spends countless hours poring through historical archives, old blueprints, and oral histories—looking for forgotten stories that explain what lingers in abandoned jails, Victorian mansions, and forested ruins. This fusion of research and fieldwork shapes his unique storytelling voice: one that weaves together emotion, mystery, and truth.

Outside of work and writing, Derrick is a proud husband and father, deeply grounded by his wife, Tara, and their two daughters, Lily and Grace. A lifelong hockey fan and certified coach, he finds clarity and camaraderie on the ice, where focus and discipline mirror the intensity of paranormal fieldwork.

Through every chapter and every case file, Derrick Smith invites readers to reconsider what they think they know—to listen closer, dig deeper, and never stop asking questions

# Books by Un-X Media

**Haunted Independence Missouri** by Margie Kay 2016
**Gateway to the Dead**: A Ghost Hunter's Field Guide by Margie Kay 2016
**Family Secrets** by Jean Walker 2017
**The Kansas City UFO Flaps** by Margie Kay 2017
**Un-X News Magazine** 2011-2025 in print and digital
**A Sonoma County Phenomenon**: **Evidence for an Interdimensional Gateway** by Margie Kay 2019
**The Fast Movers: Evidence for High-Speed UFOs/UAPs** by Margie Kay, Bill Spicer, and Larry Tyree 2020
**Journey to Spirit** by Devin Listrom 2020
**Winged Aliens** by Margie Kay 2021
**The Remote-Viewing Workbook** by Margie Kay 2019 (on LULU)
**The Master Dowsers Chart Book** by Margie Kay 2021 (on LULU)
**Rules for Goddesses** by Margie Kay 1999
**The Alien Colonization of Earth's Waterways** by Debbie Ziegelmeyer 2021
**50<sup>th</sup> Anniversary of the SE Missouri Ozarks UFO Flap** by Debbie Ziegelmeyer and Margie Kay 2022
**Meeting Wallace** by Larry Costa 2023
**Poems by Pat Delap** by Pat Delap 2025
**Holiday Poems and Recipes by** James Bair 2023
**Adult Coloring Books** for meditation by M.K. 2023 -2005
**Earth's Unseen Inhabitants** by Larry Tyree, Bill Spicer and Lily Nova
**Incident in Varginha: Space Creatures in the South of Minas** by Vitório Pacaccini and Fernanda Pires 2025
**How To Research a Haunted House** by Margie Kay and Violet Wisdom 2025
**All Monsters are Human** by Derrick Smith 2025

*Coming soon*:
**Missouri: UFO Hot Spot** by Missouri MUFON 2025
**THOR: The Extraterrestrial on Earth** by Margie Kay 2025
**Upgrade for Humons** by Peleg Yagen 2025

**Documentary Films:**
PORTALS; The Cube; Mysterious Missouri
And more!

Un-X Media is seeking authors who write books about unexplained phenomena, alternative health, and esoteric knowledge. Contact us at www.unxmedia.com for more information. Un-X Media and the Un-X Broadcasting Network are subsidiaries of HearthMasters, Inc.